Ella Frears is a writer and poet based in London. Her debut collection *Shine, Darling* was shortlisted for the Forward Prize for Best First Collection, and the T. S. Eliot Prize for Poetry. She has held residencies and fellowships for the Tate Gallery, the National Trust, Royal Holloway University physics department, John Hansard Gallery, the Dartington Trust, 16 motorway service stations, the number 17 bus in Southampton, and Exeter University's environmental history department. *Goodlord*, is shortlisted for The Forward Prize and a Sky Arts Award for Breakthrough Artist of the Year. Ella is a current Royal Literary Fund Fellow at the Courtauld Institute of Art and hosts *Tears for Frears* on Soho Radio.

T03492850

Also by Ella Frears

Shine, Darling

GOODLORD

AN EMAIL

ELLA FREARS

corsair

CORSAIR

First published in Great Britain in 2024 by Rough Trade Books
This paperback edition published in 2025 by Corsair

1 3 5 7 9 10 8 6 4 2

A CIP catalogue record for this book
is available from the British Library.

ISBN: 978-1-4721-5961-8

Design by Eliza Hart and Craig Oldham at Office Of Craig

Printed and bound in Great Britain by Clays Ltd, Elcograf S.p.A.

Papers used by Corsair are from well-managed forests
and other responsible sources.

Corsair
An imprint of
Little, Brown Book Group
Carmelite House
50 Victoria Embankment
London EC4Y 0DZ

The authorised representative
in the EEA is
Hachette Ireland
8 Castlecourt Centre
Dublin 15, D15 XTP3, Ireland
(email: info@hbgi.ie)

An Hachette UK Company
www.hachette.co.uk

www.littlebrown.co.uk

We're delighted to be renewing your tenancy. We've partnered with Goodlord, a property technology company, so you can sign your renewal contract online. To get started, you'll need to set up an account with Goodlord.

Ava, Nestor Estate Agents

Dear Ava,

It's not your fault this caught me like it did –
Goodlord – the name disturbs me most. As though
we're meant to pledge ourselves, to call our faceless
landlord *good...* or *God,* and I should – should I? –
feel graced, or blessed to live under this roof?

Oh Ava, I was snagged on it.
To tell the truth a thread came loose,
I should explain:

picture me in this little flat you rent us, lips
parted, blowing my coffee's meniscus into waves – soft
at first, then crashing up the mug's insides
and over,

yes, the sheets will surely stain,

and I was thinking of the old gods, Ava,
and ships they sank without notice, without malice,

I was reading an article, just the top, peeking
over the paywall; the surface-foam of current events
lifted with a teaspoon,

the surface is where the art is, I said.
Not everything's like coffee, he replied.

I like my men bitter.

It's been a while since we've – well,
we did have thrush – *a pox
on both our crotches!* – see, Ava,

the article spoke of basements being built across the city

3

they can't go up,
and so they dig

I think that was the gist but

what intrigued me most was the idea that
once they'd dug – what – three floors down?
the digger was too big to get back out,

cheaper then, it said,
to dig a little grave and bury it there – imagine!
Thousands of diggers entombed across the city...

you must have many questions but I only read the tip
of it,

it struck me though,

and I thought about the summer's day
a surveyor friend, well, more-than-friend,

let me climb into a digger's little cab and pull the earth
from deep inside a trench,

a thrill!

Perhaps you've also tried,

I made a joke, a good one,
about burying a body, then my phone rang –

my uncle had died.

All those diggers sealed in concrete, underground,
so sad,

and then your email, Ava,

and though it was a Sunday,
that soft buzz is like a siren's call – I couldn't help but tap
the icon,

I was in bed.

Did I mention that? Lazy, you might think, but
I'd had this dream...

I was wandering through a house I visit
often, though I've never actually been.

The Big House, I call it.
The grand construction of my sleep.

It's funny,

but I've never dreamed of here – this little flat – though
it's – what, nine years now? –

you'd know.

I suppose these boxy multi-purpose rooms don't suit
the architecture of dreams.

The Big House has winding halls, and grounds,
and countless rooms that shift,

shall I show you around?

Might be nice to take a tour yourself, no?

Come on in,

observe the polished concrete floors, the
big bay windows, and that view! The stars and planets
swimming – the universe in perpetual bloom,

and inside, my previous day unfolding
                    like a fern,

look there!

        You might think that's my granny on the carpet,
in child's pose, but things change in the peripherals,
stare directly and you'll see she is in fact
a rotisserie chicken.

            Ava, speak to it,

                    it might speak back! And tell you all about
its chicken life, that ended in
                    my kitchen –

that reminds me,

            Re: my previous emails about the oven, Ava,

how we have to stick a chopstick through the back
and manually spin the fan like cranking an old car to
make it work,

            all those emails to your office...

the dodgy lock,
                        the rising damp,

that swollen crack across the worktop – Ava, I can't bear
to press it!

Though it's begging to be pressed

and no reply until this email, Ava,

Goodlord

that closed compound, enough to
make me housesick, how I hate it!

Hated him too, first time we met

that surveyor more-than-friend

it was winter,

I was queueing at the cinema, lost
in thought, I was thinking about dogs – the extra things
they see and smell and hear beyond our reach...

He wanted to get by, I hadn't seen,

and so he moved me with the rolled-up newspaper
in his hand.

Startled – shifted – I looked at the paper
rolled-up tight, then at his eyes, cold, already locked
ahead and moving past me and I was sure, that in that
moment, I had thought so deeply of dogs

I'd transformed.

Ava, please don't stress, I know pets aren't
allowed here – honestly,

I've never even known a dog.

Once when I was walking home I saw
a small, quite fluffy dog beside its owner.

As I passed I met its eye and thought,

what a stupid little face,

I heard my brain annunciate the words, my mouth,
of course, was closed.

The dog began to bark, tugging on its lead,
gnashing its tiny teeth, growling...

The owner was shocked,

she's never done this to anyone before.

Is there a digger under your house, Ava?

Hard not to think of them like buried pets.
Not dogs, but diplodocuses their arms like long necks,
raised.

Thousands of machine graves.

That uncle – my uncle – was an impressive man,
bodily I mean, broad and tall. A brick. A house.

His wife was mean and small.

They put his coffin on a gurney,
I guess to save his friends the struggle.

It looked odd to me,
I much prefer the carrying of men by men –

the gravity.

My uncle's small, mean wife wore lace.
She'd paced about the house waiting for the hearse as
though about to go on stage.

The cemetery was on this steep, steep slope,
    ankles buckling in their black-heeled shoes.

The greyest sea beyond, the houses far below.
    Everything to the side of grief. Even the sun
beside the point, you know?

    The priest was young, I'd watched him
kiss the book and thought the kiss a little wet for death.

Anyway,
      the undertaker almost lost the gurney
to the slope.

    I willed it, I confess!

    To speed past your small, mean widow and her
ghoulish friends, and shoot over the edge, to make one
final joke, refuse the grave they'd dug for you,
take flight –
    now there's a death!

Do you believe in ghosts?

    You must, Ava. I don't.

And yet I have seen two.
    Seen one, heard another.

As a child, whenever I had a fever, I'd hallucinate:

clocks, where no clocks were, the hands spinning
at a weird speed, too fast but also sort of... lagging.

It's common, I've heard, in children – maybe you used to
see things too.

Sometimes I'd see the ceiling gently falling in,

a train hurtling towards me – much too fast... and yet
too slow.

During one especially bad night, my mother called
a doctor. He asked to speak to me, she handed me the phone.

What can you see? He asked. He had an accent, maybe
French.

A train, I whispered.

What you need to do, darling, he said, *is board that train.*

'Darling' – I know!

No doctor's ever been as tender since!

Thing is, Ava, it worked. I never saw the train, or clocks,
or ceiling
coming down again.

That doctor's voice became a talisman of sorts, you see –
do you? – where I'm going with this...

whenever I was overwhelmed, I'd feel that weird
speed push me forwards, drag me
back,
and I'd play
his voice
inside my head, *darling*
board that train...
and everything
would settle,
Ava,
do you
understand,
for years
I comforted
myself with *darling,*
board that train,
and then
offhand
one day
I told the story
at a dinner
that my mother
was also at
and after, quietly
she said, *no*
that never
happened,
no night
doctor,
no sweet, French
doctor, just you,
a child with a fever,
speaking
in an accent
we had never heard

before. Quite
spooky, actually,
she said,
one's child calling
herself
darling
like that –

           Ava, what the fuck.

Better for me to say he was a ghost, than unpick that
tapestry,

           though rich, I'm sure.

Actually,

           the dream I'd had before your email moved
my phone across the bedside table with a buzz –

I could hear him in the basement of The Big House,
the sweet French doctor, I could hear him through the
floor, but couldn't find the stairs or door

           to get to him.

           I asked the other people there – party guests,
all wearing masks that bore the faces of my favourite
people fixed in disappointment, I felt sweaty –

           I guess it's on my mind... I mean –
I'm trying this new deodorant out,

           a natural one – have you gone through this phase
yet, Ava? You know those spray ones kill the planet or
your breasts –

it's pretty herbal this one, intensely so

and though I'm not so sure it's any nicer than the smell
of me... I persevere.

I must have worn it in my dream while looking for the
doctor because a figure with my mother's face sniffed
and asked,

have you been marinating pork?

...sage, citrus, rosemary leaf oil...

I am the pork.

And still the doctor called me from the basement,

darling... darling...

but I couldn't find the stairs
or door –

in horror films the basement is where monsters are.

I lived in someone's basement for about a year,

it wasn't you – was it? – The letting agent
for that place?

I hope not, Ava.

I've never been so frantically unhappy!

Corridors so narrow that my shoulders touched
both walls as I walked down, my bedroom had no

window – a sort of breeze block coffin, just bigger than a
double bed.

No window!

Just a plastic door onto a small communal courtyard,
concrete too,

not much out there, except a washing line,
an old fridge drawer with someone's strawberry plants.

The basement flat next door to mine was
occupied by women – *a brothel!* – I was told by a
particularly sour man upstairs.

I doubt it's true. And anyway

what does it matter, Ava, they were sweet and quiet,
they had these kids there, twins I think – a boy and girl,
what – three years old? – who'd play outside my door.

See, in the summer I would have to keep it open or I'd
bake,
and so I'd have a curtain drawn across,

at this time I was going out a lot,

nocturnal,

summer's days I'd nap, the ceiling creaking
with the heavy shuffle of that sour man upstairs,
the fabric of my curtain gently billowing in the
dusty breeze

and often I'd be woken by a scrabbling
sound and see four tiny arms reach underneath the
curtain,
feel around for anything on my floor,
and if there was an object, they would take it –

a make-up brush,
a pair of plastic sunglasses,
a tangerine,
a mug,
a postcard from my aunt,
countless bobby pins
and hairbands...

I never stopped them.

Instead, began to feel quite superstitious about the
things I dropped.

I'd never pick them up.

Libations.

Once it was my favourite lipstick... I saw it hit the
floor and roll towards the curtain, and felt happy

to be free of it.

What even is a *property technology*, Ava?

Goodlord.

It's always been a triangle – us,
and you, the shapeless, shadowy form that is
our landlord.

Goodlord.

Maybe they are like God

landlords.

You never use his name, just *landlord* –

your landlord –

as in...

*"This email is to inform you that your landlord will
be increasing rent."*

Remember that one, Ava?
A classic!

Interesting, it wasn't that
that set me off –

no we just shuddered, muttered, took it

it's how things are.

But this –

I read your email and a strange, chilled anger
filled me, Ava,

like if fury were gazpacho – zingy, fresh,
and icy –

brimming

oh

        it's spilling over –

Ava, I refuse

            to stem it –

I've known this feeling once before

        cool rage

      evening dress

          captain's hat

bass deep light dimming strobe ceiling low jump glass
warm alcohol sweetening wood sticky wet towel laughter
cheering skin tightening brain thinned knee rising blood-
impact ring imprint tooth dislodging clean blur clean blur
clean – but here,

        I'm falling into something else, it's not for you,
this,

        not yet, Ava –

        I want clarity.

I want to be so clear with you

and look –

        I haven't even told you how we met,
that surveyor more-than-friend and I –

        met properly, I mean.

After the cinema, the newspaper,

woof woof

I was working in a pub, a gastropub –
      it had a pizza oven, Ava.

I wasn't in the basement yet.

My first year living in a city.
First year at University.

      In halls, we were sixteen to every kitchen.

It was chaos,

      but a dream, Ava!

The books stacked up – the Post-its on the pinboard.
Carpet tiles and yellow pine and flaking paint –
Oh hi there, sweet Nostalgia! – the cakey hobs, the partly
melted plastic chopping board, the jagged knives.
The toaster that would spark and make your crumpet
taste *un peu toxique.*

      Our floor was mostly art students

            and so the bath in the shared
bathroom would frequently be filled with eggs

      or oil

or blood – though fake I think, or animal at least –

or cream.

No one ever cleaned it with anything but water so
it had this ring – this film – a muddiness in the grain of
the enamel. Sort of purple, if purple were unhappy.

And still we bathed, Ava!

Candle on the windowsill, beer swigged from the
bottle
                                    and sometimes a friend or lover
would be in there,

                        crammed together
                        in the grime.

Sure, our deposits never made it home.

But they're not meant to are they, Ava?

First week, I walked around with my C.V.

and this pub hired me on the spot.

A girl in halls had told me – *print your C.V. in navy
blue instead of black so it stands out,*

                        I did.

And then one night the surveyor and his friends
came in while I was working –

                                    thing is, Ava, I'd never
normally entertain a man like him, but this pub – was
kind of dodgy –

                        I wasn't exactly thinking straight –

how do I put this?

I was young, nineteen –

you're not much older are you, Ava?

Twenty? Twenty-two?

I've looked you up –

and all the other people working at this bar were men –

some boyish, some more grizzled, some
completely addled – fucked!

This pub was owned by a big brewery – I forget the
name – a chain – who never checked on things,

they never came to see how it was run,

or hadn't yet

and boss-less, boundary-less, these men had lost the
plot –
a night-time world of booze, free money
from the till, and girls and girls and girls just coming in.

At first I found it funny, Ava, the way men are
when left unchecked together.

I liked how I became the centre of the orbit
working there

all glances led to me

my body.   Hot.

Thing was, I needed the job,

    and these boys,

                they had a bet to see
                who'd fuck me first.

Really, Ava!

Though I didn't know it then.

    What started as gentle flirting, well,

it escalated
        fast.

    And though some of them were cute – especially
this curly-headed boy who smelled so good... the rest
were kind of gross, and one guy – Matthew –

well, he was really mean.

    I giggled through a week or two.

    The work itself was great – a busy bar, the rush of
keeping up, and all the happy, horny eyes of strangers.

    With the bar between us, I was safe.

I loved to pull a pint with eyes locked on the eyes of a
student, banker, hairdresser, local alcoholic, then move
on to the next.

You might be thinking I was up for it,

I was.

I'd pin the bits of paper, napkin, cards with people's
numbers, names, and little notes onto the pinboard in my
room – near-conquests! what-could've-beens!

There, I was *Woman*. Born from egg.
Gazed upon, adored, fought over, stolen –

I felt indestructible.

They'd have these lock-ins after work.

The manager was rarely there at shift time but after
closing he'd emerge. He had this office like a cupboard,
would sit and watch the footage from the cameras.

He was pallid, wormy-thin, I guess
in his late thirties – soft, sad eyes.

The only one who didn't try it on with me. In fact,
I seemed invisible to him.

Slightly disconcerting.

He had girlfriends on and off.

Once, when I was working on the daytime shift, a
girlfriend came for lunch. She was about his age, looked
sensible and clean. They sat and had a pizza and a
cappuccino each. They were cuddled-up inside the
leather booth, I took their plates, they barely noticed me,

and then I saw his hand move up her thigh,
she laughed and slapped it,

Grandad, no!

So that's what he was into.

Anyway, these lock-ins, they felt fun, the way
it can be fun to dip a toe into the dark, cold water of a
lake you'd never swim in.

I felt sciencey – you know that feeling, Ava?
Like doing field work

not that I've ever worked in science you
understand –

but I've often felt my brain
switch, put on a lab coat and observe.

Fourteen I think, was when I felt it first – some
boys from school had asked to see my breasts.

I showed them. I didn't see why not.

We were by the reservoir, just out of town.
T-shirt raised, I watched them take me in. Time slowed. I
shivered and the bushes shivered too.

It was a trade – a swap. They got their
willies out. I took them in right back. Their corduroys,
dicks in hand, the muddy path, the cowpat by their feet.

That cloudy sky was really trying to
have a golden hour...

then two weeks later, I was walking home just after dark with another boy, who was my friend – a soft, large boy who had an Eeyore quality – and he told me that the boys had told him what we'd done.

You'll show them but you won't show me? He said.
Why would you want to see? I asked him,

but he sulked and said we couldn't be friends.

And so, I did what I had done before, because why not, Ava? I lifted my shirt for him to see. But he immediately bent down, began to lick my nipples.

That's when my brain put on the lab coat first.

I thought, *it's happening, so why not study it.*

What can you feel? I asked myself.

Very little, was the answer – streetlamp, tarmac, geraniums in a window box – *cold... and weary for my age.*

There was no trade – he showed me nothing in return, left triumphantly.

Later watching *Ground Force* with my mum, I got a text from him.

Did I take advantage?

Oh Eeyore! I still don't know! The thought hadn't even
crossed my mind. And when I didn't reply another text
came through.

I had to stoop.

Anyway Ava,

the lock-ins at this pub – they had my brain
wearing that lab coat almost all the time – I didn't mind.

After closing up, with all the lights switched
off, the bar wiped down, the guys would rack up lines.

The chef, an older Polish guy – who
hated pizza but made the best I've ever tried – would
have the drugs, or else he needed to pick up –

and so often this bloke, Ketamine Chris, was there –
he'd turn up, hang around – he was tall, quite buff, with
long eyelashes that if the light was right made him look
film star pretty,

but he moved in this erratic way – an aggressive
clumsiness. His eyes were scary wild.

He was from Johannesburg,

would say – *you English babies with your knife
crime, and your milky tea.*

He had a tattoo that said TECHNO right across his neck.

His jokes were weird, surreal – they never landed but all
the guys would laugh,

and if the manager was single, or feeling single, he'd bring his laptop out, and him and a few other men would scroll an escort site pointing, jostling.

Matthew would say,

     that one's a dog,

request a girl with   *zero flab*

     And the curly-headed guy who always smelled so good would shove him gently,

     are you joking, Matt? I pray for dimples on a woman's back.

     A few women would show up.

     Mostly I left early.

Once I got so stoned the hours slipped by and I was there slumped in a booth, a couple of the guys still chatting round me, while the manager fucked an escort at the back

     they were by the waiter's station, her hands gripped and slipped on the pile of laminated menus.

One time they thought it would be funny if I chose which women they should get. I scrolled through cleavage, ribbon, lace, and blurred face after face after face.

What's your type?

     I didn't stay to see the girls arrive.

That night, I let a nerdy boy I didn't fancy kiss me in the
halls kitchen. I'm not sure why. He tasted of cheese toasty.
One of those nice guys who'll try and finger you
immediately and when you gently push his hand away,
he droops his face – a sad dog with crumpled skin – and
says, *girls never want me.*

There's a specific touch of the waist one does,
Ava, when working in a busy bar, to pass behind –

a touch that keeps us flowing like a dance –
fridge, to taps, to optics, to the glass washer – oh! The
greasy, boozy steam of the glass washer!

Have you known it?

That rising cloud both sweet and
sour embedded like an anchor in my mind, I feel it,
taste it now...

That waist-touch, Ava,

began to linger.

And then if I was bending
down to get a pint glass from a shelf, I'd feel a crotch
press in behind me.

Or if I was standing at the taps and
someone needed something from that shelf, they'd reach
right through my legs.

I had these tights the curly-headed guy had said
he liked – like fishnets but the holes were flowers – I'd
wear them every time I knew he was on shift.

Good girl, he'd say when I walked in.

I loved to flirt with him.

He had a girlfriend who'd come in from time to time.

To me she seemed quite old – as I imagine I might, if we met – oh will we meet, Ava?

This girlfriend seemed put upon and stressy, he told me she was pressing for a baby.

Twelve years, they'd been together,

an eternity, I said.

It's really not, you know, he shook his head, *just makes it harder to get out of.*

God, he smelled so good, Ava.

Matthew would see me flirting with the curly-headed guy and glare and grab me roughly as he passed.

And I'd say *hey!*

                           but in a 1950s way.

Coquettish.

And he'd whisper – *you love it* – loudly, wetly in my ear.

Ava, I know this sounds so stupid, but I thought I had it covered.

There was this older grizzled alcoholic who worked there
too called Arthur – never touched me, Ava – more
interested in drinking.

He taught me how to pull the perfect pint so he
could neck the demonstrations – various pints with
various heads.

He played the protective father most of the time.
Would step in if a customer was rude.

By closing time, he'd be quite drunk,
would drop things, undercharge for drinks and the
manager would get pissed off.

Arthur would act up to try and win him back.

He'd talk about the women in that night,
and if that didn't work, would turn to me as I was wiping
down the bar and say,

lads, what colour do you think her nipples are? Are
they big and puffy, love? Go on, get 'em out.

And if they laughed, he was off the hook.

I'd laugh too.

You've got to laugh, Ava,
you know that,

we know that.

I'd lasted three months by this point –

quite the feat.

One lock-in, we were all jammed in the
leather booth, I was squashed between the window and
Ketamine Chris who was holding court as he racked-up,
he was talking about anal sex – *arse fucking* – and how
this girl shit on him once, and how he kicked her out.

At some point he zoned into me, trapped there
against him and he put his arm round me and said,

you're clean aren't you, babe.

The others shifted, looked unsettled, *Chris...*
but he glanced up at them,

a flash,

two flick knives opening – I swear
they even made that sound, Ava – his eyes.

The boys went quiet, continued skinning-up.

Don't worry, I know exactly what they like, he said
batting his eyelashes like a cartoon cow,

and then he leaned in close and bit my neck.

Quite hard.

I panicked – *I need a wee!*

You'll have to climb across, he said still on my neck.

I was wearing those flower tights and little denim shorts.

As I climbed he jammed his hand under the shorts, but
couldn't quite get in – thank God for the sturdy weave of
a good quality gusset, eh, Ava!

In dernier we trust.

Next day, I was back at work.

The daytime shift is boring in a pub.

A few sad, lonely men, who barely have the heart
to stare at you,
but do.

Matthew was hungover, coming down.

He'd been there that previous night until the sun came
up, he seemed a little cross,

you'll really flirt with anyone won't you.

He was mostly on his phone.

I dried wine glasses, hung them by their stems.

I was wearing the same denim shorts.

> *Don't you own any other clothes?*
> *You know they're way too tight,*
> *right up your vag, I bet they stink.*

And then he said the barrel needed changing
on the ale,

I don't know how, I said.

He looked pissed off. *Christ, you dopey bitch*
I'll show you.

And down we went into the basement of the bar. Damp
yeasty smell, the metal barrels everywhere.

I felt it coming.

I'm sure you know it too, Ava – that spooky feeling, just
before things take a turn.

No cameras in the basement. Just one way out.

I didn't stand a chance.

...darling, board that train...

I guess he won the bet.

It was that evening, Ava, the surveyor more-than-friend
came in.

A group of men in suits.

They paid in cash. I saw their wads and was impressed.

I know.

They played darts, drank wine, misheard my name
and called me Jane, invited me to play,

– go on, Jane! They shouted.

I threw my three darts badly – it's better for the tips.

And he, the surveyor in their midst, was quiet, moody, I knew his face of course. He barely seemed to notice I was there. Surprise, surprise.

He whistled for the bill.

But when he paid, he slipped his business card to me. *Why don't you call me, Jane.*

You see, how these things happen.

Are your colleagues kind?

Thing is, Ava, sometimes an unkind man can be a laugh. Sometimes it's fucking hot, you know?

The surveyor had a Masters in City Planning. Was obsessed with order, cleanliness – *clean lines* – he loved concrete. Like, *loved* it.

Miracle sauce, he called it.

It never fully cures, he told me once while I was on all fours, *it just keeps hardening forever,*

keeps getting stronger forever

harder forever

stronger   and harder

harder

     and harder

  harder –

      oh, but Ava I fear I've made that
gastropub sound grim.

I did have fun there,
    loads of fun before the –

   this one night – I'd been working there about a
month – we had a lock-in that was pretty jolly,

lines of coke,

   quite Christmassy,

   and all the cuter guys were being cute. Old curly-
boy was telling me he thought I was the type of girl you
could play golf with –

     isn't that sweet?

I thought,
    they've really got it made, these boys.
They've built a kingdom for themselves,

   were giddy with it.

I'd probably be the same.

The chef made extra pizzas, brought them out, the
manager let us choose our drinks from the top shelf.

    And there was no talk of escorts,
no Ketamine Chris.

Someone put some music on, and one lad, the KP –
a *Star Wars* fan – had a stormtrooper mask in his bag,

they found it, teased him, got it out and
passed it round.

Everyone had to do a funny little dance.

Real laughter, Ava, you know the crying kind.

So great.

And then the manager said,

it's her turn,

and he handed me the mask.

I want a lap dance, he said.

And I thought –

> *this! This is what you want?*
> *The man in charge, could ask for anything*
> *and this is what you want?*

And with the mask on, I could only see the shapes
of them, like shadows in a dream. I moved my hips – the
music slow and bassy – and I felt their laughter soften to
a solid velvet quiet around me as I snaked my body up
and down.

I thought how stupid it must look to
someone walking by and peering through the window – a
stormtrooper with the body of a teenage girl – twisting,
winding, with ten men of various ages stood around just
watching.

I turned my back to him and hovered moving just above his lap, back and forth, so slow I barely moved. His hands were tentatively at my waist, the lightest touch.

And when the song had finished, and I, grinning, pulled the mask off,

their faces were so sweet, sincere,

pure admiration, awe,

they looked like little boys,

...that was really good

You see, Ava?

It's so silly it will break your heart sometimes.

Goodlord Goodlord Goodlord

I'm sure I'd find this funny too, if everything were different.

Am I mad?

I did start making an account, Ava. I'm not a total psychopath,

I thought – *just let it go!*

Just sign-up to the thing and sign the contract and be done with all of this.

I mean really,

      what's another platform.

            Another password.

                  Another website with my

information.

              Goodlord

I had to wait,

           input a five-digit code sent to me via text.

When it came through it was:

              00000

      which seems insane.

I stared at it for more than my allotted minutes.

      Goodlord

That's implausible, is it not?

      Like aren't those numbers random, Ava?

How is it that I found myself with all those holes?

      A row of ohs.   Disgusting.

No, I can't go on.

      I won't.

Do you watch porn?

I ask, Ava, because I think it says
a lot about a person, what they watch,

like recently

these videos where girls get 'stuck' have had me
thinking – you know the ones? Where girls are doing
laundry and get stuck somehow inside the washing
machine – their heads or arms are trapped inside, and
just their bottom-half sticks out, they call for help, a man
or men show up, and they get fucked –

I find the flimsy artifice of every woman's
stuck-ness very pleasing, Ava,

you can clearly see she's snagged on absolutely
nothing.

Sometimes she'll even come unstuck mid-fuck and
hastily shove her arms back in –

the narrative shifts,
the plot thickens to a roux.

One time at the surveyor's house, he left his
laptop on while he was showering and I scrolled about a
bit – looked at his history.

He'd searched the web for

"bitch gets tamped"

but the search had come up empty.

—did you mean:

      "bitch gets slammed"
      "bitch gets smashed"
      "Tampa bitches"
      "bitch gets her tampon stuck"

      ...

Imagine, Ava, a kink so niche it's not been catered for.

He'd watched these YouTube videos instead for hours
of concrete being pumped – an endless stream,
a flurry of slurry – the men in hardhats muddied
to their hips, tools in hand to rake and smooth
and tamp.

      Makes sense, he fucked like he was trying
to flatten me.

      Talked like it too.

Do you think those porn actors feel sciencey during shoots?

      Sometimes they do wear lab coats in their films.
Those ones are pretty dull though.

I'd like to know what you watch.
      What thrills you.

      Surely some revelation is at hand;

Do you know that poem, Ava? You really should.

I thought of it, the day I got your email, hadn't crossed
my mind since we studied it in class.

Back then it didn't strike me,
but when your email cut across my misty post-dream
thoughts, this poem sparked before my eyes –

my mind's eyes,

as though Yeats were shouting at the
windows of my soul –

I clicked reply,

typed back to you without much thought –

> *Turning and turning in the widening gyre*
> *The falcon cannot hear the falconer;*

I didn't press send.
Perhaps I should have,

perhaps that's all that's needed here.

It might have saved you hours of reading. If you're
reading –

are you with me still?

The falcon cannot hear the falconer;

I knew an estate agent once, long time ago,

when I was just a simple seaside girl – she was the
daughter of a farmer, had a creamy face, high ponytail.

I'd started seeing someone just a little older than I
was – though a small age gap can be cavernous when
you're young – and Ava – was I!

This woman was a friend of his, I think they'd also
dated once.

She sort of took me in. As though I were an
urchin – needed schooling, caring for.

She was posher than the rest of them, land-rich.
Had owned a pony, been to competitions as a child so
seemed caught between the wilderness of their world,
their friends, and the land of jodhpurs.

She'd buy me drinks, chastise me for my outfits,
my behaviour, tell me I should stand up straight,

and when I slouched, or made a joke she thought
unsavoury, she'd reach behind my head as though about
to stroke my hair but, checking no one saw,
would grip a chunk and pull
in one fast movement,
hard – a real tug,
so that my head jerked
back, and whisper
NO!

Quite fascinating, Ava.

I let her do it.
I sort of didn't mind.

I felt she wanted to harm me further, but in a sexy way,
and that, Ava, was interesting to me.

It was a heady time! The blustery moors. The crackle of a bonfire on a hill. The cold Atlantic!

It's good to know the strength of water early, don't you think? To be a tiny child tugged under, tossed about, mouth full of salt and sand.

I think it puts things in perspective.

Oh, the countryside, its buttery truth!

My father was a swineherd. Mother was a seer of sorts.

Have you been marinating pork?

That creamy-faced estate agent disapproved of everything, but then her friends were pretty scrappy, pretty wild –

I loved them.

Especially my slightly older guy.

He lived in a tall house by the docks with a few other men.

The house was old and beautiful, rundown of course. Big windows with a big sea view that nobody, including me, would bother looking through.

Have you seen the lichen on those roofs, Ava?

It's orange.

I heard you only get that type of lichen when the air is really clean.

Farewell to that quite soon I bet!

This guy that I was seeing was warm and easy – strong – paint-flecked,

no haircut exactly, just his hair the way it happened to be growing after someone shaved it.

No particular style of clothes – he seemed dressed in what he'd been given or had found.

He was a little baffled by my outfits,

What are those?

Wet-look leggings

Wet look?

Wet-look.

Wet look?

First time we slept together he slapped his dick gently, weightily against my body, thrice –

slap slap slap

and I said,

no need to knock, just come right in.

I think I loved him, Ava.

He had no covers on his bedding, just a bare mattress, the innards of the duvet, pillows.

It's like a cloud, he'd say.

I'd recently had the coil put in – have you had one
before, Ava? Maybe you have one now – it's fine, it
works, but no one tells you that it hurts when it's put in –

Christ! I nearly blacked-out!

I'd been spotting for about two weeks, but had been
careful not to let him see.

One night though, I forgot to slip a tampon
in post-sex and woke up with a little spot of blood there
on the mattress.

He was fast asleep.

The shame! It's not like I could strip the bed and wash
the sheets!

Can you imagine?

I thought – my only option is to cut my thigh and say,

Oh, look! I must have scratched myself while sleeping.

I didn't do it, Ava, of course not – my nails were
far too bitten back.

I woke him up, and in a nervous little voice
explained the situation.

He rolled over and went back to sleep.
The stain was there for weeks.

His apathy felt tender, Ava, sweet.

I got to know his housemates slowly –

in the room next-door to his
there was this fisherman – scallops I think – with silver
hair.

He'd gone grey at sixteen – it made him look
distinguished. Otherworldly.

He hardly spoke.

He had this haunted quality. Misty-eyed. Seemed
elsewhere often. Someone told me that he had found a
body in his net, hauled it from the sea.

Not that he mentioned it to anyone – but someone
saw it in the local paper, showed the others. They never
told him that they knew.

Sometimes coming home from partying,
the light about to break,

I'd see him, in his work clothes
heading out, he'd nod, but all he'd say was,

dawn.

And then there was a tree surgeon they called 'the sex
pest', who had the attic room – he'd try to grab you if
you found yourself alone with him.

Sounds bad, Ava, but it was sort of fun.

As soon as whoever else was in the room had left,
he'd turn dramatically, slow motion, like a father who's
about to tickle a child

and you would giggle, run.

It was widely known he couldn't get it up.

And so the threat seemed dulled – a pencil not a knife.
A poke and not a stab.

You follow me?

He'd go for anyone – whatever shape or age or gender,
you'd get grabbed. Which kind of made it better? – More
democratic, maybe?

And he was handsome, so you wouldn't run that fast.

Would you pull my hair when no one's looking, Ava?

In the room beside the bathroom
was an accountant they called Percy – though that
wasn't his actual name.

He was small and bald with rosy cheeks –
cherubic with a smoker's cough, a girlish giggle.

Most of them had met in school but he had joined them
later. Seemed at odds with them.

They'd often hold him like a battering ram and use
his head to smash a wardrobe or a chest of drawers.

One time, when he had passed out drunk,
they gaffer-taped him to a plastic chair and put him in
the garden.

The next morning, he was exactly as they'd
left him –

fast asleep. Serene.

They sowed grass seed into his bedroom carpet and
then watered it – it grew.

And when he locked his bedroom door to keep them out,
they took it off its hinges, burnt it.

I sensed he welcomed each new torture, but I couldn't
work out why.

He was in love with an older barmaid
in the pub just down the road. She was gay. It didn't
seem to bother him. In fact I think that's why he'd
chosen her to love.

He held his soft devotion like a penance –
drank alone, admired her chastely, monklike in the corner
of the pub.

I don't think that he ever told her.

I never saw him even glance at anyone else.

The others in the house told me he
used to have long hair, but one summer while working in
a factory as a teen, he'd caught it in a drill and scalped
himself.

One time I walked in on him on the toilet.
He was reading *Les Fleurs du Mal*.

Can you read French? I asked him later.

He giggled, he coughed, he shrugged.
He suggested we all brand him with a burning log.

There was another man who lived there for
a bit who owned a bar in town.

The bar was in the basement of his uncle's
restaurant – small and sweaty. All the booze was far too
sweet.

This bar guy was obsessed with sleaze. His room
had framed porn on the walls, his king-size bed had
satin sheets – gold, Ava – he had a matching robe he'd
throw on if a girl was round. He'd grown himself the
wispiest moustache –

but you could tell his heart just wasn't in it.

He tried too hard.

He had this Excel spreadsheet of every girl he'd slept
with – or even kissed – it had their name, what they'd
done and where, a photo if he had one.

He could pull up data, like how many blowjobs
he'd had that month and how many of those girls had
swallowed.

It's not like anyone was asking.

They called him Snake Boy. He had an
anthropology degree. When he was high his tongue
would dart out of the corners of his mouth.

It's fun, knowing a man who owns a bar,
until it's not.

Cool rage. Deep shame.
Captain's hat –

No.

Well look, I've drawn you to the bottom
of my barrel once again, Ava.

Thing is, the women in that group were
possibly the most fucked up.

Just take our creamy, hair-pulling friend.

And then there were these sisters, Ava,

the oldest was the girlfriend of the tree
surgeon – 'the sex pest' – the middle sister was with the
fisherman,
the youngest was even younger than I was
so wasn't dating but would hang around.

All three looked like they were lifted from a surfing
catalogue – long blonde hair, ankle bracelets, petite
tattoos. They sort of floated round the house,

always together.

I'd walk into the living room and see the three of them all cuddled up across the sofa watching *Masterchef*. Their boyfriends silent, separate on the other chairs.

I wanted what they had. Silky beauty, perfect skin, a disinterest in everything but one another.

Once when I was out in town, I saw the youngest, barefoot, walking with a goat tied to a little piece of rope.

I followed her. She walked it to the pier, sat on the edge, feet dangling down, the goat just stood beside her. Calm. And from her pocket she pulled a packet of Doritos. One by one, she fed them to the goat.

The boat masts rattled like a twinkle all around her.

The sun was bright and warm.

And then one night my boyfriend, a little high, told me they slept together – all of them – the sisters and their boyfriends and whoever else.

Orgies.

He said the sisters kissed and more, even when the guys had gone to bed.

Ridiculous, right? I thought that too, Ava – the kind of rumour that you'd spread to knock them down a peg,

only, I couldn't help but think about it,
wonder how it was and why, I couldn't shake it from my
mind –

and then one night while I was dancing in a club
the oldest sister kissed me. Long and hard. I felt this
sudden surge of something – overwhelming – grip me –
and lip-bitten, enthralled,

I realised that I wanted – needed – to kiss them all.

Back at the tall house later, the music thumping in
the kitchen, the sea silvery and cold outside the window,
I felt that urge increase,

I was in this sort of frenzied fog.

My brain was not a brain, it was a beating heart right at
my temples, pressing at the walls of me.

I went in search of them.

I've never felt desire like that before or since.

I went from room to room to room,

I climbed the stairs right to the top

and when I softly pushed the attic door,

I saw them

three beige snakes.

A knot.

Darling—

and all the want drained from me
and a nausea that I'm yet to shake
coursed through my body

and I ran.

I left the house.

And shortly after, left that town for good.

Do you think I really saw them, Ava?

It's easier to say I've misremembered.
Or that I was in a trance –

but open any door inside The Big House and
you'll see them too. They're under every rock out in the
garden. Clear as day.

Want is such a slippery customer.

For instance, I want to hurt you, Ava.

Or wanted to.

That dream I had, the day your email moved my
phone across the table with a buzz –

what do you think it was?

The thing the sweet French doctor was calling me to
find.

All these rooms I've occupied.
     I hate to walk you through them,

      though I must.

I think I should have never left the countryside.
     The mackerel on the barbecue,
          the clean, clean air. That big sea view.

     The real estate's quite good down there.

You've probably been on holiday – ice cream, pasty, surf
school, rock pool – not calling you a basic bitch,

     but Ava, you do wear Karen Millen.

Happy birthday by the way,

     I saw your post this morning.

You know the first thing that I noticed when I looked you
up is that you're thinner than I am?

     Isn't that the worst?

It's hard to keep it in sometimes. The hate. The hurt.

     Last week, I was walking through the city, fast,
was marching to a meeting, completely lost in thought
and passed two women interacting with a large stone
frog outside a restaurant.

     They were patting it and hugging it,

laughing,

pretending to agree with it – all quite lovely really –
wholesome fun.

But as I passed I caught the eye of one of them and her
face fell.

Embarrassed, she dropped her hand that had
been pressed against the frog's stone brow as though
checking for a fever,

and gloomily, they went inside.

What had my face said, Ava?

My legs had carried me quickly on, but I wanted
to go back and say,

Madam you misread me! Please! Enjoy the frog!

It stung, Ava. I thought of it a lot.

Do you have many friends?

I couldn't hold one down,

kept falling out
kept moving on

I had a friend in school with the same name as me.

It bound us, Ava, twinned us – changed the way
we were with others when together,

name twins

in twos your stock goes up,

        a plural, safe – the self concealed within
dual selves.

She and I
               did all the normal girlhood stuff together –

        we huddled,

we imagined,
               lay on our stomachs on the beach

read from the same magazine,

        fake-tanned each other,

           drew tattoos in biro on our wrists,

made up dance routines and songs,

        wrestled under the gunnera at the local pond

ate strawberry laces

           played hide and seek

took turns to suffocate the other with a sofa cushion,

        rode BMXs,
                 dived off the rocks,

and once I pushed her in a wheelbarrow through the
town, a ribbon round her neck, calling,

girl for sale! girl for sale!

I played the flute back then – I know, Ava!
   Just call me Pan – though it was tourists
not my flock we serenaded,
      her on the clarinet.

A little money tossed our way to spend on gum –
chewing... bubble...

      gum was quite important at that time, Ava,

         I should explain –

see, schools are made to teach sex-ed these days, by
law – I think that's good – no nonsense, bits and bobs,
mechanics, risks, how it all works, condom on a banana,
done –

         but we got none of that.

None of the teachers in our school would volunteer to
take the class, and so the job was farmed-out to an
eager party,

      Ambassadors for Christ

a local group.

         No, really,

      it wasn't even a religious school.

The *AFC* came in one afternoon – we'd seen them once
or twice before, promoting their events in our
assemblies.

They had this old school bus they travelled
round in with a library in the back, and on the side it said:

THE G-SUS BUS

almost as bad as *Goodlord,* Ava...

the main guy was known as Mr C., an ancient man –
that's how he seemed – older than the world –

benevolent cloudy face, hair like the finest
morning mist, arthritic hands forever rested in a chapel
shape.

And often he was joined by Faith, a fierce woman,
thin and tall, who could have been ancient too but also,
maybe – twenty-five?

She spoke once of her former life,
heroin etc.

dirt

she called it,

*I injected dirt, let dirt inside me, hung around with
dirt and so was dirt myself.*

Writing it here, she sounds quite cool, but her
delivery was so uptight, so highly strung and righteous
that you kind of just switched off when she was on.

One afternoon, we all filed in from lunch, shoving, giggling, crisp crumbs on our jumpers, backpacks low and bouncing as we walked,

once inside Faith gave us each a piece of chewing gum – now, Ava, I don't need to tell you what a thrill this would have been – gum was banned in school of course...

every small occurrence is a big event when in that barren stretch of education,

like one time Amy King sat on a chair and it collapsed beneath her

I think we laughed for months.

She had to take a week off school.

Another time a Science Clown came in to teach us physics on a unicycle and he got hard and then was asked to leave –

oh Ava, what a spectacle! His multicoloured parachute pants, his personal big top...

We drove a boy called Samuel to insanity one winter just by chanting his first name in every gap of Wham's "Last Christmas", as in –

Last Christmas I gave you my heart, – SAMUEL – but the very next day, – SAMUEL – you gave it away, – SAMUEL –

he bashed his head against the wall so hard he cracked his skull.

They called an assembly one day –
just the girls – as someone had been wiping their used
tampon all along the corridor walls.

The headmaster said he'd find out
who was doing such disgusting things to our beloved
building and they'd be expelled.

I don't think they ever found the culprit.

Good on her, I say, Ava,

whatever she was going through,
she'd found a way to say it. Made her mark.

L'écriture féminine

est nécessaire, non, Ava?

All girls who had their periods were told to queue
for questioning,

I didn't have mine yet,

still queued though, obviously,

we all did,

even those too young to be suspected –

I am Spartacus

no one wanting to admit they hadn't
reached that milestone yet.

Yes Yes, I am woman. Born from egg. Bloody enough to
endure whatever awaits me in this room.

Oh Ava, those years at school are
sealed beneath so thick a lacquer that even that week
failed to crack the surface.

Boredom on the tennis court

boredom with a bunsen burner

weekly planner

sad sandwich

mock exam

boredom vacuum forming a soap dish

reading *Our Exploits at West Poley* – of all the books they
could have taught!

Anyway, *AFC* came in one day,

we filed into the Elliott Hut – did you
have one at your school, Ava? – A sort of temporary
cabin in use for fifteen years and counting,

wind whistling through the plastic windows,

coats on kids!

and in that flimsy room, we happily chewed our
gum while listening to Mr C. explain that this was

SEX-ED.

Then Faith went round the room with a Tupperware box,
asked us to spit our gum into it,

we obliged.

Some lads did big dramatic gobs – strings
of saliva, phlegm – we squealed with horror
and delight.

Once she had this giant soggy mound of greyish
chewed-up gum, Faith went back round and offered it to
each of us again.

Here, why don't you try a little. The box thrust
right beneath our noses.

Of course we all refused dramatically.

Gross!

Gag!

No!

It whipped us into quite the frenzy, Ava,

and there was Faith,

standing at the centre of our chaos,
shining, upright – a bolt – a beam – a shaft of sunlight
breaking through the clouds onto a stormy sea...

THAT – she said quivering like a preacher, box aloft –

IS WHAT SEX IS LIKE.

and that was it – sex-ed.

I still can't put a condom on correctly.

Inevitably perhaps,

chewing gum took on this lore,
                    mysterious and seedy

we became obsessed with it –

            chewing rebelliously open-mouthed,

                        swapping it when we kissed for dares,

pressing the old gum under desks – feeling all wild and
grubby.
                        Hot.

Oh, Ava!

        Just the scent of spearmint on a person's breath,
however old, can send me – still – into the throws of
early stirring,
                        and I will never not unwrap a brand
new packet with a certain sense of ceremony.

        And so the coins tossed to us by the tourists
for our, frankly turgid, *Pachelbel's Canon,*

            bought us gum

                which we chewed

                            and gossiped
about what we thought the rest involved, and blew

pink bubbles – big as we could – and dared ourselves
to make them touch, and pierced them with our
fingers so they burst across our faces... being young
is weird, huh, Ava?

But listen – when you're in these little Portakabin
classrooms and your world is very small and you're
reading a book chosen from the curriculum by a worn-
out, weary man because it's short. You're bound to fuck
about a bit.

Our Exploits at West Poley – honestly.

If you're thinking you should look it up, I wouldn't, Ava –
one of Hardy's lesser works.

Two boys explore a cave and redirect a stream which,
unbeknownst to them, deprives their hometown of a river
far below while also prompting celebrations in a
neighbouring town who find themselves now blessed
with water for their mill.

It grinds along. The boys switch that river back
and forth... *the opposite of error is error still!*

There's a character called the Man who had Failed who
appears sporadically to muse and offer wisdom to the
boys – an obvious cipher –

why am I bothering to explain?

An education sets you up – primes you for the world... or
should, right?

What, then, did that book set us up for, Ava?

At that age, things stick –

what I'm trying to say is –

this book, read slowly, painfully aloud by
each of us in turn for weeks,

rendered my starved, reluctant brain

a cave

dark and deep

with two boys trapped inside

the water rising.

Oh look, Ava!

One boy takes off his hat, fits a candle to it and,
reaching down, he sends it out along the swirling current
looking for an escape,

little boat – throwing its warmth across the cavern
as it travels out, out, out –

stalactites loom,
minerals glint

antechambers yawn in and out
of darkness

out out out
goes the candle

from those boys
           trapped on the pitch-black ledge
at the base of my memory,

           and still the water rises.

See, Hardy might have let those boys escape,
unscathed.

           I won't.

Goodlord. Goodlord. Goodlord.

I can't breathe.

           No, I'm breathing – just

my breath is short, Ava,

           as though I'm drowning.

Not the cave, forget the cave.

           There are these buses –
                      minibuses

that park outside our window.

           Between their jobs the drivers sit there
on their phones, engines idling away – oh, this idyll
that you rent us, Ava!

...chug chug chug

Each morning I take my coffee to our modest window,
watch the buses park and re-park down below like
livestock grazing out beyond the ha-ha.

Sometimes the drivers piss against the wall just
over there – so oft' I'll see a dick emerging from a
tracksuit like the season's earliest mushroom.

Do you know, Ava, how bad these fumes are for
your lungs and heart and mind? I didn't until last year
when I read about it on my phone and as I read my chest
began to tighten, and I felt the last near-decade of those
buses chug-chug-chugging crushing in.

Before I read that article I felt fine, Ava.

It's reading that's the menace, not the fumes.

Now when I hear that *chug chug chug*

my breath gets short,

Am I dying?

I mean –

am I dying faster here than if I lived in some
well-lit, well-built, well-ventilated house?
A garden out the back –

a garden at both ends, why not!

chug chug chug...

I'm at war with them.

The buses –

of course I am.

With my Post-it notes,

my firm agitation of the blinds,

my steely glare.

I know, I know,

I'm far too young and hot to spend my evenings
noting down their number plates –

yet, here we are,

calling up the council to complain.

It eases things a little, Ava – to lodge, to file, to
oppose...

a little paperwork, a little email chain, a little
someone at a desk somewhere putting me on hold.

The hold-music for the council's parking office is
Maria Callas singing "Vissi d'arte" from Tosca.
What emotion – *che bella*, Ava!

Although those high notes through a
crackly line are piercing – really test your nerve...

it's possible that's the point.

I have to turn the phone off speakerphone before her final ardent, long – *Signor* – else I get a headache.

Goodlord Goodcall Badair

I wish I could report these fruit flies, Ava.

They drift about my vision undeterred –

peppy, is how I would describe them,

unconscionably buoyant,

apparently unkillable.

Where do they even come from, Ava?

The fruit itself?

Emerging from the forehead of a Granny Smith?

Surely not!

I'm tired, Ava.

I sneak out with my Post-it notes at midnight, when the buses are asleep – stick one to every windscreen,

You're killing us! You're killing us! You're killing us!

Those little boys deep in my cave-brain beat their fists against rock.

Goodgod that Hardy book was dire.

As was that school, Ava.

A couple of the parents did complain of course –
after the *AFC/sex-ed* debacle – felt their children should
have information, questions answered, facts.

So the school put a suggestion box in the
doorway to the hall where anyone could leave a question
about sex,

and the following week another special assembly
was called to tackle all those questions in one go.

And because no teacher volunteered, they
all were made to do it – all had to go on stage and pull a
card out of the box and answer best they could.

They sat nervously, our teachers,

and the power drained from them,

flowed down to us –

electric and enormous – we were one
embodied mass.

Our maths teacher was first to pick – a tall man with a
swirly quiff who all the mums were fans of. His voice was
low – a bassiness so silky that it must have been
affected. He used to call us *mini guys*. As in –

OK, turn to page 18, mini guys.

He pulled a card out of the box, ran a hand through his thick hair, unfolded it, and speaking with a seriousness that already had us stifling a giggle, he said:

OK, settle down – first question:

> *What is... a double-ended dild–   oh.*

Yep.

We were gone – mass hysterics. Tears, thigh slapping, can-barely-catch-your-breath laughing.

Can you imagine, Ava!

They had to end it there. What a golden day!

And all the mystery of sex preserved.

Gum and spit and shame and bicorn beasts – oh my!

That poor maths teacher though...
forever tainted.

Every lesson that he taught thereafter, haunted by the spectre of that fateful card he'd pulled.

The double-ended dildo at the feast.

Fuck. Fuck. Fuck.
Why must I sign via *Goodlord,* Ava?

Why. Why. Why.

It screws us both – the system – in the end,

and there's a point when *streamlined*
becomes *slippery* my flat-letting friend.

Are we friends?

We're different, you and I, I think –

my school friend and I were different too,
despite our names –

she'd set her sights on travel, medicine or
aid-work – had researched charities she wanted to be
part of.

We went together to a fundraiser for Médecins
Sans Frontières, eagerly she spoke to glowing boys with
lanyards, clipboards, worthy as a seeded loaf each one.

What a drag!

I wanted cigar smoke in a tent.
I wanted mud and salt and selfishness.

There was a boy in school who was in love with her –
though she had little interest in anyone back then.

One night down at the beach – big bonfire,
Smirnoff Ice – he talked and talked to me about his love
for her – her eyes and hair and beret.
I waited patiently
then when there was a pause,

I kissed him.

It was clumsy, boring, he looked furious – stood up and
brushed the sand off of his jeans dramatically.

You're not her, he said,

as if I didn't know.

She was the sweeter, softer one of us,
found my eagerness for life a little jarring.

Why would you kiss him though? She asked me. *You
don't like him either.*

I guess we'd begun to drift apart already, before my
summer in the tall house by the docks.

I'd been staying there about a month,

was missing home and so convinced her to come over
for a party they were having.

It was fun. We danced and danced,

played through the roster of our in-jokes,
swigged our beers, made-out with one another for a
group of lads because they asked us to.

Twins! Kissing!

We laughed until we cried.

They had this game they played at parties there – *The
Yellow Phonebook of Death.*

They'd take it in turns to hold the Yellow Pages
against a body part – arm or leg... extra points for face
or crotch – then someone else would run at them, a giant
hunting knife in hand, and plunge it deep into the book –
hard as they could.

Honestly, it was great to watch.

Legitimately dangerous. There were always wounds.
They played it topless, Ava.

Even my friend found it most rousing.

She was drawn to Snake Boy that night – he'd done
volunteering with a charity in India once, or said he had.

They hooked up. She passed out naked in his satin
sheets.

At some point later in the night he took a few guys
in to have a look, lifted the covers for them to see her
lying there.

I knew, Ava.

I saw them all go in. But he assured me they just looked
and didn't touch.

Next morning she and I sat on the
doorstep in the early sun – drank tea, breathed in the
cold grass smell, the brisk sea air beyond,

and she was happy, Ava –
said that he was sweet, had told her she was pretty, fun
and cool. Had kissed her neck, had checked that she

was fine, had taken things so slowly – she had liked it.
Mostly.

What would have been the point then, Ava, to have said?

I hugged her tight. She took the next train home.

The opposite of error is error still. Fuck off Hardy.

Snake Boy was lost – there was this fear behind
his eyes that made it difficult to be angry with him. Every
movement seemed performed...

thing is,

you do a thing – however unconvincingly –

you've still done it, right?

It wasn't until years later
I realised that the tall house by the docks belonged to
him,

it wasn't until years later
I heard he had a film of her as well –

evening dress
captain's hat,

light dimming strobe ceiling
low warm wood wet towel skin thinning brain tightened
knee rising blood-impact blood-impact tooth print ring
print – *you bitch you can't* – evening dress captain's hat
you bitch you can't just – ah,

well here we are again, Ava,

and all I really want to say is – well, it's never this.

They don't teach you that kind of stuff in school,
do they?

Can't put on a condom correctly.
Can't navigate a friendship.
I'm terrified of HMRC.

But I do know what an oxbow lake is, Ava;
and which of Henry's wives was pig-dog-ugly;
and what those plucky boys of *West Poley* fame stuck to
their faces to disguise themselves as wizards.

Horsehair, Ava.

This email is an oxbow lake

and I
am pig-dog-ugly too

have lost my shine, I think.
As will you.

We lost touch, this friend and I,

not long after her dalliance with Snake Boy – perhaps
she sensed that I was keeping things from her, or she
regretted the encounter anyway.

Maybe she felt stifled by our
twinning – understood our fundamental differences, the
arbitrary basis of our bond.

I wanted to stay friends.

I'd felt her slipping, held on tighter, texted her long
messages with all our in-jokes shoehorned in.

Like a desperate lover, Ava,

no, not *like* – I did love her, I was desperate.

She'd got a job in Vietnam – a big adventure,
a fresh start,

I worried she'd forget me,

so I ordered her a mug –

printed with a shiny photo
montage: us together through the years – smiles, fancy
dress, tongues out, beers raised...

I chose too many.

It was ugly and chaotic – friendship propaganda.

Forced.

The last time I saw her, just before she left, I had it
in my bag to give her but the atmosphere felt off.

She seemed impatient – rushed a bit to finish our
goodbyes, said it would be hard to keep in touch but
that she'd try.

I kept that mug tucked in my bedroom drawer for
when we reunited – a funny story to add to our
collection,

my ugly gift, my ugly love...

but when, months later, I saw online that her and
her new housemate out in Vietnam had matching tattoos
of a key – their key – I threw it out.

Though first, destroyed it – obviously. Rolling pin in hand,
mug wrapped in kitchen roll,

I smashed it with the focus of a murderer
dispatching with a victim's teeth.

Do you have a best friend, Ava?

You seem the type.

You'll have a group – a gang, no doubt.

I thought I'd find a new friend via circumstance – thrown
together in the maelstrom of chaotic campus life,

but I never gelled with housemates, classmates...
anyone in that way.

Bad luck perhaps,

badgirl

badfriend.

I had run away from halls and the gastropub to live as
Jane.

Had left my stint as nice, clean Jane in the
surveyor's nice, clean house because I'd heard some
girls from class were looking for someone to move in
with them.

I didn't say goodbye to him – just slipped out once he'd left for work. He never called or texted to ask why, or where –

our time was but a blip, Ava!

I do think of it warmly, though,

or tepidly at least.

He was distant, sure –

he tolerated me – got angry if I made the slightest noise or mess – but here's the thing, Ava – I wanted to be small and soulless for a bit,

and honestly, I even liked the sex.

Pummelled flat, face down

tugged under, tossed about, mouth full of salt and sand... Poseidon, is that you old friend?

A lovely flatline of a summer.

And all the concrete dirty-talk was kind of hot once you got into it –

volumetric   *asphalt*   *reinforced*

Is there letting agent dirty-talk, Ava?
Are you a *cosy one-bed?* Bet you are.

Bet we could jam another occupant or two in at a push...

Anyway,

      I saw this girl from class say that they needed
someone to move in last minute and that was it –
I jumped ship –

      swam off to Girl House like the little rat I was.

I am.

      Girl House.

         Six of us in one big terraced home –

      the biggest bedroom that I've ever had – a chest
of drawers, a mirror leaning up against the wall, a bed,
and nothing else except the bare magnolia, big sash
window, great expanse of what was once green carpet,
faded to a brownish grey.

I liked those girls, Ava,

         but they already had a friendship formed in
first year – anecdotes of freshers' week, of club nights,
parties, festivals that previous summer, all the lovers won
and lost, and though I really tried I couldn't work out
where I fitted in. Their in-jokes made me chilly, and my
shivering killed their laughter dead.

      I was their Percy.

I would have let them brand me with a burning log, Ava,

if only!

No,

I pretended to have other friends and plans
to save them having to include me all the time.

I'm sure they knew.

I was working as a waitress in a restaurant down
the road – Colombian Fusion.

My boss was this neurotic woman in her forties,
gym-obsessed from Somerset, who owned the business
with her husband and his mother who was the chef.

She would say –

He's the Colombian, I'm the fusion!

All the time.

She'd also look me up and down and say

a hundred squats a day would change your life.

She requested that I sweetly sing – *hola!* – when anyone
came in.

We had Colombian customers of course. They winced at
this, peered past me to the kitchen to make sure.

A few days into working there my boss confided
she was having an affair – she'd started sleeping with the
owner of a rival restaurant down the road.

Italian place. Italian man.

He'd pop by occasionally – drink a beer, chat to the husband or to me while she served tables hip-ily – coming back to shake the cocktail shaker in a way that made her tits bounce quite chaotically.

Ciao baby! She'd say to him. *We're always glad to have the competition over,* and she'd ruffle her husband's hair and kiss him on the head while holding the Italian's eye.

She was obsessed with being obsessed.

Would ask me endless questions –

Did I think that she was bad?

Is it wrong to want to have a little fun?

Who did I think was better looking – her husband or Francesco?

Didn't I think she was in better shape right now than in this photo of her twenty years ago?

I gave up sugar – feel how soft my skin is!

and I would touch her arm or cheek and say –

oh wow, like silk!

She'd show me texts from him to her.

We'd analyse the tone, discuss what she should text him back.

She'd ask which lingerie I thought that she should wear, which 'saucy photo' she should send.

There was something strangely sexless about it all.

In the photos that he sent, his dick looked sad and stoic as though trying to keep its head held high under enormous pressure – basically it looked like Atlas, Ava. Sans the globe.

Once, she had me watch a video she'd made for him –

her sitting opposite a mirror – sliding her underwear to the side, slapping herself between her legs repeatedly. The sound was sort of comical, like someone slapping steak. Her face reflected in the mirror made an exaggerated *oooh*.

What do you think? She asked me earnestly.

Sure, yeah... hot. I said.

She told me that before she met her husband she had worked in an Ann Summers –

men like it when I tell them that, she said, *I used to use the sex toys in the storeroom, put them back into their packets without washing them.*

The empanadas there were excellent.

I'd take a tray of what they had leftover home to Girl House every Sunday night.

We had a lot of parties at that house – good space
for it – big and bare.

My favourite housemate there was Molly – on the
art degree.

Her hair was always pinned in these elaborate
styles – faux-pearls and feathers strung across – and
with it she'd wear leg warmers, T-shirts, neon netted
gloves,
        the kind of style that has you and your
colleagues raising eyebrows, Ava.
        It's different to be fair...
                You lot with your blazers and your patent
heels, Ava,
                I would stamp on you,
                        I really would...

Her boyfriend called her Molly Antoinette.
He was around a lot.

Tall and lean. Face aloof – vaguely angelic. From money
but hid it pretty well, though occasionally he used his
Latin.
        Equo ne credite, Ava.

We were all impressed by him for two reasons:

First:
                he made his own trousers. Rough
patchworks of silk, low-slung. When he stretched his
arms up – which he did a lot – you saw his lower
abdomen, sometimes a little fuzz – not quite the top of
his dick but it was definitely there...

and second:

he had a criminal record for throwing stew –
specifically cassoulet – at a pro-life protester near a
clinic.

His social media bio had a little emoji of a fist.

We thanked him for his service.

Molly made art about what she called,
radical partying.

For her first 'group crit' she gave each person in
the class a card that read:

You're cordially invited to my consciousness party

and had them sit in silence for
her presentation time.

In the feedback part, the tutor was apoplectic,
could hardly get her words out –

It's... lazy! It's... lame!
It's lazy and lame!

Molly was unfazed.

She spent the next few months creating giant party
props – enormous cakes, big paper cups, plates,
balloons and streamers...

her project culminated in a string of giant
bunting, two hundred metres long.

The triangles were tall and wide – stretched from floor to ceiling. She wound it round and round throughout the house and we embraced our newly festive lives.

Bunting cut across each bedroom, made a theatre of our beds.

Two triangles flagged the toilet,
one trailed in the bath.

You had to be careful running down the stairs to get the door in case you self-garrotted on a ribbon.

In the kitchen, we'd brush them to the side with wide arm-sweeps like explorers parting vines to find the kettle.
It was weird, Ava, but leant a softness to the house that I quite liked.

One day behind a bunting curtain, I found Molly crying. Her boyfriend had suggested that they *open their relationship up... let other people in...*

She was desolate
then angry –

he's not that great, you know! She said.
And then she told me these three things:

One:
that she had thought he really fancied her in sunglasses because of the intense, romantic way he gazed at her whenever she put some on – but that recently

she'd realised that it is, in fact,
the face he makes when gazing
at himself.

Two:
that he liked her to pretend to be
asleep – or dead – when they were having sex.

And three:
the pro-life protester who he'd
thrown cassoulet over, had a baby strapped to her.
And that his actual crime, the part
he never mentioned, was not assaulting her
but her baby.

The narrative shifts!
The plot thickens like a stew.

...a fucking baby.

I watched her sob into her yoghurt.

That evening she agreed to his new terms.

And on they went, together, *open,*
though she wasn't seeing anyone else.

He was.

When she agreed with him, or stroked his hair,
or cooked him dinner,
he'd say –

that's why you're my favourite.

Have you been 'open' ever, Ava?

I'd be surprised.

It's never appealed to me –

the upkeep, the inevitable soreness, the jealousy.

Once I was invited to a party by an American
student in my class – a few years older, wealthy,
shiny flat right on the river –

city view – *views*, Ava, plural.

He was throwing a thanksgiving thing –

to cure my homesick heart, he said.

He'd worked at his dad's restaurant in L.A.,
I figured he could cook.

I'd love to come, I said.

He smiled.

And if you have a friendly friend, he said... *the more
the merrier.*

I was curious, I confess, Ava.

I knew he and his girlfriend liked to go to
those kinds of parties.

I didn't fancy him –

a sort of postlapsarian jock – expensive
crewnecks, healthy tan, thick hair but with rebellious
additions – chipped black nails, eyeliner, leather bangles
fraying on his wrist.

His girlfriend was a buoyant sociology student –
dyed red hair, the word *boobs* tattooed in neat, small
letters on her chest.

I took a dish of sweet potato dauphinoise,

added it to the heaving table – enormous
turkey at its centre.

So glad you came! He said and handed me a
whiskey cocktail the likes of which I've never tasted
since – sweet ambrosia, Ava – lethal nectar.

I chatted to the various couples,
ate a plate of food. The gravy was exquisite.
The city glowed around us.

We ate and talked and ate.

Full and sober now, I sat on the sofa, sipped my
drink. Looked out the window at the river glistening
down below.

Everyone else was standing in little groups,
politely talking.

The host's girlfriend put some music on,
whooped, took off her top and bra and shimmied round
the room.

A few groups of people stopped their talking,
watched.

One guy said, *Weyy!*

Another nodded with appreciation
        but no one joined her in her dance
                or semi-nakedness.

She saw me sitting on the sofa on my own and laughed,

don't be shy babe, come and dance, she said, I
shook my head,

she looked uncomfortably around, her boyfriend
wasn't in the room, I'd seen him slip off with two women
early on.

Come on, she said again, more forceful.

I felt bad but smiled and shook my head again.

She tried that lasso move on me, I grimaced
apologetically, remained unmoved.

The room was a bit bright, I thought, for this,
and I was far too full to want to be observed.

She seemed more naked than she had before.
I thought I saw her shiver, considered offering her my
jumper.

She looked worried, *come onnnn,*

a little desperate,
then her face turned cross – determined.

She strode across the room defiantly,
straddled me on the sofa
and began to kiss me
roughly.

A little cheer went up behind her in the room.

Perhaps this is how all these kinds of parties
start – I wouldn't know.

The kiss felt much less certain than I'd expected,
considering the force with which she'd boarded me –

fumbling, frightened almost, she seemed keen for
my mouth, my tongue to take control and I was thrown
back to a memory from primary school – sitting in a
circle under a big pine tree down at the bottom of the
field, the ground compacted – brown and dusty, strewn
with needles – taking it in turns to kiss each other on the
mouth. Wet, familial, curious – a game like any other –
rounders, barefoot, long jump, daisies plucked,
beheaded with a thumbnail, stones bashed on other
stones to make a chalky powder, doctor, patient, storm
the castle, strip the red hot pokers of their petals, jump
from one slab to another, forty-forty I see, tadpole! there!
tadpole with legs! dizzy, spun around and fell and grass
stain on my knee, hot graze, dark grit stuck to it, and a
girl with messy hair and snotty nose her graceless mouth
hits mine, and sticks, or is it me, the girl, my mouth now
focused dutifully on – who?
    I pulled away

boobs – the word was in my face.
Around us party guests were feeling one another up.

Shall we go upstairs and see who's in the
bedroom? She whispered.

Right behind you, I said and left the flat.

But what a flat it was, Ava!

Most impressive of erections – panoramic views,
throbbing city, river coursing filthily below...

I wonder do you ever get to manage listings sleek
as that, Ava?

Well,
if this flat that we rent from you is anything
to go by – no.

I may be trapped in the eternal off-white quagmire
of chipped ply, rising damp, and dodgy curtain rails,

but so are you, I think, Ava.

It was around that time a lecturer handed
me a book as I was leaving class.

Read this, he said.

I read the blurb when I got home – a teacher becomes
obsessed with his new student and they begin a doomed
affair.

I left it on my shelf unread –

I just could not be
fucked, Ava, to lift that veil,

transparent as it was already.

He never mentioned it again.

If you're feeling short-changed by this one, Ava, I agree.

It's not like me to let the waters of desire
trickle past undrunk – but his approach was so risk-free,
so non-committal...

Nah.

You'll never find a teacher-student situation in my
search history, Ava.

Yawnsville.

Hey – that would be a great name for a
company if Molly's boyfriend ever started making porn.

Post bunting installation the parties that we threw
at Girl House didn't work.

No one mingled. You couldn't see who else
was there.

People danced within their separate
coloured fabric walls, got bored, and left.

Also, if the girls were on the sofa chatting
and I walked into the room they wouldn't know that I was
there unless I made a noise – cleared my throat or
something.

I snuck up on them a few times accidentally which made the awkwardness much worse for all of us.

And so I rarely left my room.

There was one girl in that house I was particularly intimidated by – we all were.

A tiny German girl – a film student with an impressive collection of designer vintage clothes.

She was a kleptomaniac.

Got caught shoplifting in M&S one time while wearing a fur coat.

They didn't call the police – she was so small and chic – her crime was so bizarre – the security guard just said,

...but you can afford parsnips..?

And let her go.

I loved her accent – the way she said vagina with a hard 'g' as in vigour.

She ate a lot of vegetables and little else.

She'd always have a pan of beetroots boiling on the hob.

She had this ancient baking tray, we weren't allowed to touch – worn and scratched, its black coating peeling off.

She thought we didn't notice but sometimes she'd
put the tray into the oven empty, then eat the bits of
coating that came loose.

The way she ate them, Ava – lifting those shards
of black – what, enamel? – Paper thin, savouring them as
though they were the rarest most delicious crisps... well,
I still think about it now,

wish I'd tried it.

She stole things in the house.

I'd hear the girls complaining that their
clothes or shoes or earrings had gone missing – though
never to her face.

She didn't take my clothes or shoes,
but she used my towel most days.

She'd take it from my room or from the washing line,
then leave it on the floor outside my door when she was
done.

I did try hiding it

but she would find it while I was out at work.

Often I'd pass her on the stairs – fresh from the
shower, defiant, squeaky-clean and tiny, my towel piled
high around her hair.
In the end I stopped resisting – resigned myself to
sharing it – I left it for her neatly folded every day.

It wasn't so bad, Ava.

She used expensive hair masks that made the
towel smell really good – I kind of hoped my hair might
get some residue.

Is that pathetic, Ava?

I think that was her magic – her residue, her glorious
dregs –

see,

just as you were at your wits' end with her,
she'd throw you something – an old designer jumper
with a moth hole at the cuff, a nearly finished bottle of
Chanel toner, a book she'd read, a ticket to an exhibition,
film, or play she couldn't make.

She did do one thing, Ava, that I found insane –

she never used her key.

She'd always ring the doorbell – whatever time of
day or night, she'd expect to be let in.

Really! As though we were her butlers.

Even this, though, wasn't quite enough to spark a
mutiny.

I asked her – *why* – once, having stumbled
out of bed at 3 am to let her in.

It's cold, my hands are numb, she said

and floated past me, disappeared into the bunting.

I guess I was quite lonely there.

I worked and read and worked and read, and stared up
at that Artex ceiling feeling mad – my phone buzzing with
messages from my boss like:

*Valentines on Sunday, dress in red AND SEXY for your
shift, I want us to be matching XoXo.*

That Valentine's night, a regular at the restaurant
handed me his card. A cosmetic doctor –

it's easy to get rid of freckles these days, he said,
we just use a little laser.

Oh Ava,

> *I should have been a pair of ragged claws*
> *scuttling across the floors of silent seas*

that's Eliot,

who won't have known an Artex ceiling,

but did know loneliness, I think.

Do you?

I'm sure of it –

I can picture you walking in your skirt suit to a
viewing, keys and folder in your handbag ready, thinking
about how you'll sell this couple in their thirties on a
grubby studio flat, eighth floor – *great views up here* –
you let them in. Gesture outwards from the centre of the
room, point at the kitchen, making sure to leave the

cupboard doors and fridge unopened – you've learned the hard way how mice droppings, forgotten food, some mould can spoil a sale. Instead you pull the door – *a little stiff!* – onto a tiny bathroom and the shower curtain billows with the sudden change in air. Sad and stained, it seems to reach for you, and you step back somewhat disgusted – though you try to make it seem as though you're making room for them to peer into the space not big enough to walk into together. They ask if they can have a moment to look round alone – *of course! Take all the time you need.* You move towards the front door then you pause – the neighbour who was just outside the flat when you came in had looked a little dodgy and you'd felt his eyes all up and down your legs when you'd walked by. Instead you pull a sliding door with all your strength onto a balcony so narrow that you have to slide in sideways, bum against the glass. Below, an ambulance is parked-up and you wonder if there's somebody inside. You check your phone. A car parks badly, blocks the road, another honks its horn impatiently. You look out across the grey buildings and squint and think about the tiny lift the three of you had crammed inside to get up to that flat – stainless steel, embossed, dented as though beaten-up – touch of the abattoir about it, *cunt* spray-painted, partly scrubbed-off, but still visible on one wall – the couple looked uneasy as the lift creaked and shuddered up the floors and you had stood in silence, though now you think you should have called it – *spacious, handy, fast* – a soft small panic flutters in your chest – *I wish I had a lift in my building,* you should have said. The wind feels mean today, it whips your hair into your eyes, your make-up feels tight and tired and waxy on your face. You look straight down. You don't consider jumping, but you do consider what it might be like to want to jump and that's enough to make

97

you nauseous, want to leave. It's awful here, you think. You want to be in bed at home, or even in the office at your desk. Not here. But then the couple poke their heads out and they tell you that they're interested and just like that you're in control again.

You switch your face from soft to hard.

There's a lot of interest. We're suggesting people put in offers to secure the flat – an extra hundred pounds a month, say, over the suggested rent should do it.

goodlord goodlord goodlord

and they do. They always do.

We would have stayed another year – at least – at Girl House, but the letting agents for that place told us last minute that we had to leave.

Do they – do you, Ava, – mean to cause such panic and unease?

Is it fun to watch us scramble to find housing?

Those stupid, lazy students with their loans, their pasta-pesto and their new opinions... is that it?

Or does it just not register as real?

I called to beg the agent, Bronagh – perhaps you've met? – to let us stay a week or two,

just while we find somewhere to live.

She hung up on me, I called right back, another agent
answered.

Bronagh's in the hospital, she said.

...but we just spoke?

And now she's in the hospital.

Thoughts and prayers for Bronagh. Grapes and flowers
for Bronagh.

We bid farewell to those sweet days of bunting.

The deposit was withheld, of course,

they said we stole the garden shed –

there is no shed! We told them.

There isn't now, they said.

They sent us photos of the garden.

In the first, a little wooden shed that we had never seen
before – adorable, painted green.

The second showed the garden as it was – empty,
overgrown. A few rogue slabs, a broken barbecue from
the house's former life.

What could we say?

How does one prove the non-existence of a shed?

The girls found smaller houses, split
their group in two.

No room for me this time.

I searched once more for anywhere, for anyone's
extra room.

The queues for viewings were down the street. Students
bid on houses they hadn't even seen.

Outside the door to one, the agent said –

*if you don't say you want this now, before you
look, it's gone. I've got another student on the phone.*

And that, Ava, is how you end up grateful for a
basement.

I took the room. Descended gladly.

Shoulders bumping both the walls as I walked down.

Goodgirl Goodgod Goodgrief

But did the shed exist?

What, Ava, is your professional opinion on the matter?

They were wily, those ones, I wouldn't put it past
them to invent a shed.

But here – I'll give you this, Ava...

I do remember, hazily, one party, glancing
out the bathroom window,

seeing a bonfire in our garden, soft flame
amid the brambles, slabs and knotweed –

what were we burning, Ava?

There's no way that we'd bought firewood –

where does one even?

No.

We burned the shed then...

well,

there is one other option:

see,

out the front of Girl House there was always a
T-board that said *LET BY* and the agency's name.

One evening, frustrated with the agents ignoring our
request to fix the shower, we felled the sign and brought
it in.

In the morning there was a brand new
board out in the garden. Upright. Triple cable-tied.

Creepy.

Very creepy, Ava.

This happened at least three times.

Therefore, it could have been the signs we burned.

If I were to kill you, Ava,

I'd build a pyre of T-boards, and I'd martyr you.

Gooddeath.

I don't think it would make a difference though –

the boards would be replaced,
as would you.

The self-healing, self-perpetuating state,
thick-skinned, amorphous – regenerating even as
we try to pierce it... why hasn't it burst yet, Ava?

The market.

It can be pleasurable to lance a boil.

We should find pleasure where we can.

What's your vice, Ava?

I had this ritual that I loved –

small, silly thing.

Every Thursday, heading home from work I'd buy a pack
of gummy-worms then eat them on the train.

A treat!

To be a woman in the world and eat
can come with complications, Ava – I know, I know – so
tired a point, it's barely worth the making, yet...

I'd cultivated a style of eating that was
unabashed –

                so effortless was my technique it rendered
me impervious to looks or judgement.

      You can't falter, Ava – that's the secret –

                      can't let them see you being
nervous or unsure... packet sandwich, shy unwrapping,
mayo on the jumper – *goodlord* no!

      I ate those gummy-worms with verve and vigour.

Mythic femme-fatale. A bag of thick, fat, sweet
invertebrates.

      Though I'll admit – even with a confidence so
carefully honed, sometimes one must forgo for safety –

      know what I mean, Ava?

Like, last summer

      I was coming home from a work trip
up in Scotland –

                  long train, over-booked, toilets out of
order – as per, as per – but I'd found a window seat –
what luck!

An old man asked if he could take the seat beside me –

but of course! I said.

He nudged my shoulder with his shoulder, *you're a lovely lady,*

and off we went.

We chatted as the train pulled from the city. I felt my inner barmaid surface, joked boisterously. He opened a can of lager, offered one to me – I declined.

Where's your food and drink? He asked. *You should eat something.*

I assured him I was fine.

He was nudging me a lot now.

Such a nice young lady.

Pretending to jostle for an armrest I was nowhere near.

You should eat something, where's your food? He asked again

and jabbed me in the ribs.

My body shifted cold. My inner barmaid shrank.

By the third can he was telling me he liked my dress, touching my thighs.

Trapped against the window, my mind was
racing – lab coat on – doing the various calculations:
how long did we have left, how brazen he might get, how
might I find a way to move or have him moved without
things getting weird or worse.

I'd noticed that his knuckles were cut and bruised. He
saw me looking.

I might be old but I can put a fella in his place... you look
hungry, love. Why don't you get a little snack out.

Four hours until my destination.

I put my headphones in, feigned sleep
against the window.

He rapped his knuckles on my head.

Hello? Hello? Let me ask you something.

I told him I was feeling claustrophobic.

You can put your legs across my lap, darling, not like
that – to relax – not like that don't get offended...

I watched the landscape rushing past outside the
window. There were tight gold bales in every field.
I felt bale-like, bound and solid and ridiculous sitting
there.
Perhaps, Ava, you're one of those women
who can just stand up and loudly call the man a pervert,
walk away. Not me.

Why aren't you eating? He croaked into my ear.

For hours, Ava, I held my thighs locked tight, arms rigid –
nodded, smiled, shook my head – while he besieged my
hair and arms and legs, poking my ribs, tapping my
shoulder, my head, placing his hand on the window while
he spoke to me so that his arm was like a rollercoaster
bar across my chest.

At one point a guard came through to check the
tickets and I sent a look that said *please help me.*

The old man asked with exaggerated frailty how
his day was going. The guard looked thrown by this and
said,

not too shabby, thanks,

then shrugged at me, moved on.

Touch, poke, jostle, grab.

A man in his late forties at the table across
the aisle – headphones, laptop – ignored my search for
friendly eyes.

By the time we pulled into the last stop, he was
drunk, his voice a gurgle, singing

pasty legs, you've got pasty legs...

I said nothing, stood up, gathered my things.

*You must be starving, love. Not even a sip of water this
whole time.*

He looked me up and down, turned to lift his
suitcase off the rack.

I saw my chance – slipped through the gap,
sped past him and along the aisle towards the door,

but an elderly woman was in the doorway
struggling to disembark, her daughter helping her slowly
down onto the platform.

I felt him catch me up.

I didn't look round.

He pressed his body into mine, buried his face
into my hair and croaked

you're a cunt.

And then the door was clear and I ran.

It felt so stupid, Ava, running from this old
man – too drunk, too frail to catch me up.

But run, I did –

up the platform, through the station, zig-
zagging through the crowds of people watching the
departures board, and out into the summer evening air.

That strange fixation on my eating, Ava – what was that?

These are the kinds of things that could deter a
girl from her indulgence in a gummy-worm or two,

which is why I took such pride in eating them,
Ava,
                        each precious Thursday evening,
          the city with its lights on, the endless office
windows, the train reflected, winding through – a worm
itself.
          Such quiet joy!

          But pride

comes before a fall, Ava.

          One happy Thursday evening, worm-in-mouth, I
glanced up – met the watchful eyes of a man
who seemed to know me,
and recognised him
with a jolt
as the first boy
that I ever blew.

          Really, Ava.

What a joke that was,

                    or should have been.

The fates were really laughing when they spun that day –

               a loop.

          As if those first encounters aren't embarrassing
enough – now I have to stack another memory on top.

          Small talk. Red face. Half-eaten worm jammed in
my pocket.

Worst part is, Ava,

       now I can't stand the gummy fuckers.

They taste like shame

       or him

or adolescence

       which is sweet
but terribly unstable,

       and with the added sugar now feels sickly,

I can't stomach even the slightest
recollection.

       Am I making sense?

       In the mirror, in the shower, on the train,
at my desk,
       in The Big House of my sleep,
I groan out loud.
       Hoping, I suppose, the sound will
scare the memory away.

       But The Big House has a groundskeeper
who rakes and rakes the same old leaves and no amount
of groaning stops his work.

       Is it the same for you, Ava?

       There must be food or drink that you can't
swallow, for the place or feeling that it pushes onto you.

It's like hot chocolate, Ava –

                              haven't drunk it since the job
I had when I was just sixteen –

      my first!

            Waitressing in a sort of bistro

wine-dark walls,

            multiple cream-based sauces on the menu.

                        Staff weren't given food, but we
were allowed to make ourselves a coffee on the coffee
machine.

I didn't like coffee then. But what I did like, Ava, was hot
chocolate.

            It was just this tub of powder, nothing fancy, but
with the milk steamer it was velvety and good.

            When it was quiet I'd spend time making a perfect
mug of it and lean against the bar and contemplate this
oil painting of a sexy señorita in a dark red dress –

                        her implausible bust was thickly rendered
with a pallet knife,

            something off about the angle of them – the
weight – a shift in genre from her figurative, almost
hyper-real face

            to a voluptuous expressionism at her chest.

I spent many an early evening, restaurant empty – waiting – studying her blankly, trying to solve the bad equation of her breasts.

One day as I was absent-mindedly sipping my hot chocolate, the boss came out –

big bloke, temper, friend of my aunt's, would often talk loudly in the open kitchen to the chefs about how good he was at *playing the pussy field* –

which – OK, fine – but the other waitress was his girlfriend and I'd have to watch her wince, pretend I hadn't heard.

Anyway, the boss came out, saw me with the mug raised to my lips and said, *are you fucking serious?*

Then yelled at me about the cost of things, and taking liberties, and how you can't be generous because your staff will always take the piss – and how many of those had I guzzled anyway on his time and money – and what else was I stealing from him – and I just stood there, Ava, dumbly – small, hot-faced, and waited for it to be over.

As he walked away I went to pour it down the sink, he saw –

What the fuck do you think you're doing? What a waste! Drink it now you've made it.

I didn't want it.

When he was gone I dutifully downed the
lot in one. Washed the cup. Went to the bathroom and
threw up.

His shouting had been relatively tame
compared to arguments I'd heard him have with the
head chef –

a hapless twenty-four year old
who'd recently lost custody so had his kids' faces
tattooed enormous, haunting, heavily shaded
on his shins.

He had a temper too – this chef.

When the boss shouted, he'd explode right
back, throw pans and loudly quit before returning the
next day to prep.

He had these terrible ideas for restaurants of his
own. He'd sit as we were opening up and tell us
endlessly about them –

his big idea, Ava,
was a restaurant that served British classics
but as sushi –

think about it, he'd say, *a full English, blended,
wrapped in rice and seaweed, cut into perfect little
mouthfuls – tell me you don't want to try that!*

Can you imagine?

Blended eggs and bacon.
Blended fish and chips.

And pie.

He also told us he was set to win the oyster
shucking competition that October,

it's in my blood, he said, *eight generations. It's just not
possible for anyone to shuck faster than I can.*

The morning after the oyster festival he came in to
pick his wages up. Both hands were heavily bandaged
and he smelled strange – sort of stale.

The Man who had Failed.

That's what they're really like, Ava,

not wandering philosophers offering wisdom to
little boys in caves.

But bumping into you in a club on a Friday night,
asking if you'll lend him a tenner then shouting,

you've got great jugs, really, I mean it,

in your ear.

Did I go home with the English-breakfast-sushi chef?

I did.

His children's doleful eyes were quite off-putting, Ava.

I kept mine shut, conjured the señorita from the
painting – it helped.

I've found she still pops up from time to time,
when I need assistance –

Goodgod.

Maybe I'm the Man who had Failed.

I'm watching you, Ava,

posting photos on your way to a friend's wedding.

I knew you had a gang!

Prosecco, silk pyjamas, hair tongs...

In my mind I'm loitering near the venue

shifty, hood up,
head down, waiting for you to arrive.

As you walk past me

I catch your arm

...there was a ship!

My weather-beaten face, my bloodshot eyes, an ugly
friendship-mug around my neck.

Goodlord. Goodlord. Goodlord.

What would I tell you?

A warning –

something about death and greed and
inspiration...

something nautical, I think –

what about the *Agamemnon* – Nelson's favourite
ship – whose birthplace I visited... and saw a ghost,

no, really, Ava.

What a mess that was.

Boatswain's Clench, the place was called –

pronounced *Bosun,* Ava, these old
words can be a trap –

Goodstock Shipshape Shipmate

a charcoal stove tried to kill me there,

at Boatswain's Clench –

it felt like everything out there was trying –

the wasps, the weather, the trees, the locals...

you see,

I'd seen an Arts Trust put a call for
applications out –

*Opportunity for low-income artists to spend eight
weeks in our magic space.*

A photo of a tiny wooden studio right on the river –
picturesque!

An artist? I hear you asking, but Ava,
it's not as big a stretch as you might think –

I'd been drawing customers and colleagues
secretly for years on the order pads at the various places
where I worked,

captioning them with small verbatim quotes –
things overheard, or just their orders

'pork and chips'

you get the gist.

I liked the order paper – rough and greyish, with
the little number at the bottom.

I'd kept them, stacks of them – and this is what I
presented to The Trust.

Post-basement, I'd been living in another
houseshare – *quelle surprise!* – a mix of strangers that I'd
found online:

a clutch of graphic designers, a chef we never
saw, a woman in TV.

A large Victorian house.

The bottom floor was a separate flat so everything felt
squeezed –

you must think that's a shame, Ava!

Some part of you *must* hate it.

These houses made specifically for living
by some New Man with Ambition marching through the
smog as one century clicks over to the next...

bought a hundred years later

by a dickhead in a shiny suit

and chopped up into flats.

Kitchens shoved in rooms that once were bathrooms.

Bathrooms added willy-nilly making
bedrooms L-shaped, odd shaped, too small, too
awkward to fit anything but a bed,

even the little attic space, however steep or
strange the angle of the ceiling, is a bedroom now.

Glossy portfolio. Buy-to-let mortgage swinging
down the street,

and every house and flat, garage and loft
decorated with

NEUTRALITY and *THRIFT*

as their main guiding principles.

Oh, Ava!

These cursèd rooms,

they sap! they sap! they sap!

Goodlord

Doesn't it depress you too? It should!

The separate flat was occupied by a couple
and their toddler and their baby. I don't know how they
all fit down there – didn't, I suppose.

There was a narrow corridor from the front door
that passed their flat and led upstairs to ours. They kept
their bikes out there.

Every day we edged around or climbed across
those bikes – oil smear on my new cream trousers,
plastic bag snagged on a pedal. Bashed shin, bashed
knee, bashed elbow...

I've never understood them, Ava – bicycles
past childhood. I'd hate to feel inferior
and sweaty on a road.

We didn't complain.

They looked exhausted all the time,

also,

when we showered it rained a little in their flat –

I think that's worse than climbing over bikes,

do you agree?

Our bit of house was on two floors.

There was a tiny kitchen but no living room, no
communal space – why have a lounge when you can fit
another bedroom in, eh, Ava?

Unless you happened to be in the
kitchen at the same time – and there wasn't room for two
of you to cook – you couldn't just hang out.

One can't get to know a stranger from the
doorway of their bedroom, Ava.

It's a shame.

We might have been good friends had architecture
allowed.

I was very nearly friends with the woman in TV.

She'd moved into the house just after me.

She had the worst room – just bigger than a cupboard
with a child's bunkbed in,

illegal, obviously –

a five bed, rented at the price point of a six bed
with a little wink-nudge from the agent...

Might as well regress a little further, said the
woman in TV when she had viewed the room.

She was tall and would have been too long
for bunkbeds, but her rent was pretty cheap.

Not cheap-cheap Ava, but –
you know.

The day that she moved in, I helped her carry some
boxes and we chatted, got on well.

When she was done unpacking she asked me if I
fancied going for a pint.

She worked behind the scenes on dating shows –
production.

Fascinating all the stuff that goes on, Ava!

The casting, the cajoling, the controlling and the *'villain
edit'* – what a notion!

Before the house share, this woman had been
dating a magician – imagine that!

His name on stage was Maestro Paul.

She hadn't fancied him at first – long
leather coat, voice a little whiney – but he'd grown
on her,

or rather – hung around enough to end up present
one night when she was drunk and lonely – swooped
on in.

He worshipped her, would tell her she was
beautiful a hundred times a day,

she'd roll over in the morning and he'd be there –
deep in some performance of arithmetic on his fingers
like a child,

                            and when she'd ask what he was
doing he would smile and say –

      just counting my blessings...

                         I know, Ava – bleak.

      But gratitude can be an aphrodisiac – she became
accustomed to it all.

        He loved her,

                                  or loved loving her –
which is the same
at first.

      Her landlord threatened to put her rent up,

so in she moved
      with Maestro Paul,
who owned his place – you see, Ava,
the things your job can drive us to?

      Beige on beige on beige with purple velour
curtains and metal skulls on all the shelves.

      It was only after she moved in,
the intensity began to wane.

He had shows, rehearsals all the time, and when he was
around he seemed annoyed by her, corrected her
grammar when she spoke.

·　　　　　　　With the love withdrawn she leaned
into that absence, filled it.

　　　　　　　Now she was coming to his shows, making
dinners that she thought he'd like, complimenting him,
crying all the time.

　　　　　　　She liked to run. Would run most mornings to
clear her head.

　　　　　　　One day, to her surprise, he asked if he could join
her. He wasn't exactly the jogging type.

　　　　　　　Shortly after they set-off he flagged, was bright
red, panting, said he had a stitch.

　　　　　　　　　He sank into the pavement. A little puddle
of a man. She felt disgusted but walked back to check
on him,

　　　　　　　he was pretending to tie his shoelace.

Are you OK, Paul? She asked.

　　　　　　　And he looked up at her all red and sweaty
said,

　　　　　　　　　　　I don't love you anymore.
　　　　　　　　　　　　I haven't for some time.

Can you believe it, Ava?

　　　　　　　He was on one fucking knee! She told me,
I thought that he was trying to propose.

So off she swiftly popped back to her mum's until
she found the room in our house – our bit of house.

Bunkbeds

    and a dose of thick, hot shame.
She was great though, Ava, I really liked her – fun and
sweary, sad in quite a powerful way – but her job meant
she had these early mornings and late nights,

        and so beyond that evening
I never really saw her much again.

  Nearly, Ava!

No cigar.

    The others in the house I only glimpsed.

  Or heard.

One of the graphic designers was called Rickie – he was
messy – handsome in a cartoon villain way.

    The toilet next to his was only used by him – tiny
toilet. Tiniest sink I've ever seen.

    That tiny sink was so encrusted with – what –
toothpaste? Spit? – it looked like something from a cave.

    He seemed nice enough,

      but almost every night in his room alone
he'd play the same video of Queen at Live Aid 1985 (full
set) full volume on repeat and sing along.

It drove me mad – it drove us all mad, I imagine.

One day I saw him in the kitchen – pasta,
marmite, block of cheddar – and asked if he could
maybe sing less loudly
            and he looked at me confused.

                    Queen..? I said.

Nothing registered, his face was blank.

            The singing?

                    Still nothing.

I left the kitchen thinking that I must have got it wrong –

            not him – not Queen – or else I'd dreamt it.

But on it went, Ava.

                    At least three times a week.

Finally I broke.

At 2 am I banged my fist against his door. Full of
sleepless rage.

            He stood there in his pants, the concert playing on
his laptop screen behind him.

He just shrugged,

            it's the last concert my mum saw before she died.

He looked good.

Sad-hot.

We hooked-up while Freddie Mercury marched up
and down the stage. Rickie's eyes were locked on him
the whole way through.

When Freddie shouted *Ayyo!*
the crowd called *Ayyo* back,
and Rickie shouted too,

Ayyo!

Eyes wet.

Quite strange, Ava, to be atop a man so thoroughly
elsewhere

but fun.

If I could rail a distant misty mountain, oh I would.

Immovable. Jagged. Icy.

Sounds sublime!

It was that night when I got back into
my own bed, I saw the call for artists and understood
that if I didn't escape that house – I too, would soon
collapse into my own karaoke-style breakdown.

The mad thing is, Ava –

I ran into Rickie years later, still looking good, still looking sad.

He was in Selfridges Christmas shopping with his mum – alive and well – so fuck knows what was actually going on there.

Anyway the Arts Trust deemed me needy, worthy of their space and, giddy with my luggage, I arrived at Boatswain's Clench –

A studio!

A room at a local B&B!

Eight weeks!

It was winter,

depth of.

I stepped out of the taxi and wandered down the hill.

No one around.

Two neat terraces of red-brick cottages flanked the sloping green down to the river where my studio was.

They were quiet, blank-eyed.

Quaint, of course, Ava – but eery.

I wonder if you know the place. Unlikely.

An eighteenth-century village on a river, on a huge estate owned by – ah, what was his name – some lord – where a few of Nelson's ships were built.

What I didn't know before I got there
                              was that it had been preserved –
a sort of fake museum village,
        you had to pay to get inside.

In the summer there were re-enactments,
costumes, old boat building demonstrations –
        but no one actually lived there. Or if they did, I
didn't see them, Ava.

                    Can you imagine, owning so much land
that you can annex-off a village, keep the thing on ice –
of course you can't.

        But really, what a life! To be a lord.

Space and deer and wild horses
and enormous houses.

                    A palace. An abbey. A wood.

On the studio door was taped the key and a note that
said, *enjoy!* signed by the chairman of The Trust.

        My heart sung, Ava.

The studio was small – wood-clad, big window, big desk,
little copper charcoal stove repurposed from a yacht.

        I shivered happily. I lit the stove.

I looked out at the muddy riverbanks, the leggy birds, the
distant swans. I got my sketchbook out and sat there
trying to absorb my new surroundings best I could.

OK, I thought. *Art.*

I drew a wobbly line across the page, then tore it out,

tried to fight the sudden boredom that was
rushing in at an appalling rate.

A slow and sickly sense of doom descended.

Why did I think that this was something that I'd like?

That I could do?

The B&B they'd booked for me was three and a
half miles from Boatswain's Clench.

The Arts Trust hadn't asked if I could drive – I can't, Ava –
can you? – And so I walked. Suitcase, miniskirt,
impractical leather boots with a little heel – a block-heel,
mind – through the forest, along the river, down the road
where cars sped wildly past me, forced me flat against
the wet and thorny hedge.

The B&B was equally deserted. Off-season.
The Trust had got a deal.

Just you and me, the owner said.

Divorcée in her sixties, brusque but kind.

She let me use the kitchen and in return I cooked enough
for her most nights – stew or soup, spaghetti bolognaise,
a pie...

It's nice to be cooked for, makes a change!

Every day it rained.

Every day I trudged the hour-fifteen out to the studio, sat there staring into space, trudged back.

There was no internet by the river.
Hardly any signal.

I saw no one.

I was yet to meet a single person from The Trust, though I'd spoken to their chairman on the phone –

...so you're our lucky artist! I'll pop by at some point – check on how you're settling in. Until then, you'll probably see me in the distance – I walk my dog round there most days.

He did.

Each day at different times, I'd see a distant figure on the hill across the river. He'd stop and turn and wave – enormous strides, deerhound, wooden walking stick – I'd wave back from the window of my studio – stove puffing away there in the drizzle, in the quiet, in the cold.

Looks cosy! He emailed me one day.

I suppose it was.

Some days, I'd time it wrong and end up walking back from the studio in the dark.

The woods were scary and on the stretch of road up to the B&B I feared for my life.

I'd been traversing the dangers of the city for so long that I'd forgotten quite how menacing the countryside can be, Ava.

Those memories returned – out on the cliffs when I was young – rosy cheeks, bouncy grass, windswept – out exploring... then suddenly that feeling, like being slapped awake – knowing you've been seen out alone.

It's how a vole must feel when spotted by a buzzard overhead, Ava.

Tuning in
        to your body with its eyes.

Meat. I'm meat. I'm meat.

Walking back to the B&B I'd hear a rustle or a twig-snap and I'd think, well this is it.

One evening after dark, I passed a dead horse in a lay-by.

Spooky lump.

I didn't approach.

It happens all the time, the owner of the B&B told me, *they're wild, protected – you can't stop them roaming – and people here drive far too fast.*

On the nights I cooked, we ate at the table in the kitchen by the Aga.

She had this boxy TV in there that was always on. It showed the split-screen footage from her CCTV.

Four little boxes, black and white, the scenes
trembled with their liveness in the dark – the garden, the
front door, the hedge and road, the pitch-black field
beyond.

We chatted, ate whichever mediocre stew I'd
made.

Tough beef.

A lamb shank clinging to its bone.

I couldn't help but watch the screen.

Behind her head a spider strung its web across
one camera's lens, shaking madly in the wind.

Some nights she went to dinner with her friends.
And I would fry an egg or else go straight to bed.

The house was huge.

It was just us there, so she'd only bothered
heating a few rooms – the kitchen, her room, mine.

Large sections of the house were freezing and
unlit.

I hated to walk past those bits – the creamy
lounge, its dead-eyed mirror; the breakfast room all laid
and ready for the spring and summer guests; the
sunroom with its wicker chairs and model ship and
magazines and sombre glass...

you know that very specific formal plush that bed and breakfasts favour, Ava? Well it's even weirder when it's frozen – held in a kind of stasis.

Each night I'd sit on my bedroom floor with my back against the radiator – outside my window was the cold, dark field, the clouded sky, the woods.

One night I saw a white horse there, awkward, ghostly.

I thought what I must look like to that horse – trapped in my yellow square, surrounded by the many empty windows of that house – a lone face watching

being watched.

It's not like I could see it looking, Ava, but I knew it was.

I asked the B&B owner at breakfast if it was a wild horse or one belonging to a farmer –

there's no horse in that field, she said a little curtly.

The carbon monoxide alarm in the studio had started going off.

I called the chairman from The Trust.

Just keep the space well ventilated,
you'll be fine! He said.

The studio window was sealed shut – it didn't open.

The door was huge – basically the whole side of the building, glass as well – I opened it, and all the heat rushed out.

I sat there freezing for a while, then walked down to the nearest pub.

This was better, Ava – fireside, people, life – a little nook to think in.

How's it going down there? The barman asked me.

Good, I said, *the river's really gorgeous, I feel very lucky.*

He raised an eyebrow.

Boatswain's Clench? You'd be surprised how many people have drowned down there – right where that studio is, he said.

How many do you think that is, Ava?

How many drownings would surprise you?

I wanted to ask, if he meant recently, or since the dawn of time.

I guess I'd be surprised if it was in the thousands...

like the diggers, Ava –

that surprised me.

There was a group of rowdy men and boys on a nearby table who overheard the barman.

They told me they were from a boat building school – one where you learn all the old techniques.

We do a couple of weeks down Boatswain's Clench, we'll come and say hello.

When I came out of the pub I had a voicemail from the chairman of The Trust.

I just walked Talbot up the hill but couldn't see you in the studio window – are you there? Do let us know if you can't use it for some reason. There are plenty of young artists who'd be happy to step in.

I walked back up to Boatswain's Clench.

Lit the stove until the alarm went off, opened the door, froze, shut it until the alarm went off, opened the door, froze… trudged back to the B&B, made soup, watched the spider busying itself on the black and white TV, sat against the radiator, peered out of the window at the strange, white horse, slept fitfully.

On the art front, I'd made nothing, Ava – had tried to draw the river,

to write about the leggy birds, the skies, the shiny mud, but my brain was empty,

achey,

dull.

The lads arrived for the boat building class.
They wandered over from whichever cottage they'd been
using as a classroom, had their lunch down by the river,
peering up at me.

I'd wave. They'd jostle one another.
Sometimes a few would knock and chat from the
doorway, attempt to flirt a little. They were either
eighteen or forty-something.

Neither appealed to me.

One forty-something guy, ex-army, showing off to
the teenagers around him, said:

Let's have your number then, Picasso.

I gave it to him.

Later sitting against the radiator, I got a text:

Alright Picasso, where r u staying?

and when I didn't reply:

it's Martin Cooper from boat building.

I googled him and found his profile – smiling with
his wife and kids. A lot of photos in his uniform with a
ruddy face,

comments underneath from other similar looking
men – *nice one Coops.*

Thirty minutes later another text came through,
playing hard 2 get?

The weather was truly miserable.

I got a cold, became convinced the stove was killing me.
I think it was, Ava.

My head felt huge, my heart felt weird, my lungs felt tight
and clogged up.

Trudging along the river the trees swung
and shook in my peripherals.

I needed paracetamol.

The shops nearby only took cash and I'd run out. I
walked four miles to a post office that had a cash
machine.

It beeped at me aggressively.

It's all out, love. We'll get some more tomorrow.

I was desperate.

The woman at the B&B found a sachet of Lemsip
in the back of one of her cupboards. I saved it for the
following day.

Caught in heavy rain it dissolved inside my pocket –
liquid lemon gold.

The alchemist of Boatswain's Clench.

I wrote down in my notebook,
                    licked the golden paste off of my fingers.

I felt shivery – cold down to my bones.

I lit the stove and stoked it up – hot as it would go.

                    A hornet woke up in the corner of the
studio, buzzed angrily, curled its sting against the glass.

          The alarm went off.

          Martin Cooper glared at me from the river's
edge, picked a big rock up and threw it in the water.

          Do I seem ungrateful, Ava?

    goodjob goodgirl bigbreak

          That night the B&B owner told me that her son
was having trouble with his baby – eight weeks old. He'd
asked her to come up to London and help out.

          *You'll be fine here won't you? You know your way
around the place, and honestly it's nice for me to know
that it's looked after while I'm gone.*

          A house all to myself, Ava.

Time and space and light and air
                              and the only thing I owed
them in return was art.

          Oh I went mad, Ava.

There was this tiny museum at Boatswain's Clench, at the top of the village.

Various tableaux with mannequins inside.

One was an old pub scene – low lit. Fibreglass figures in matted wigs, tankards, waxy jackets.

The audio was triggered when you walked into the room – a rumbling chatter of lively, gravel-voiced men, clinking, swishing liquid, humming a half-remembered tune – that tune Ava,

I don't know what it is, can't find it anywhere, it plays, it loops, I can even hear it now...

Another of the rooms contained a boat building scene – men with tools and wood and iron – a plaque to the side with an illustration of an impressive ship,

the AGAMEMNON.

The bolts alone were sixteen feet long, *forged at Boatswain's Clench*, it said.

Whoever drew the picture of the ship had angled it as though it – sorry, *she* – were cutting through the ocean at high speed,

the sails were full and strong,

cannon poised and ready,

a plethora of ropes straining –

what I'm saying, Ava, is
whoever the artist was, well, you could tell they were
very horny for this boat,

or war,

or both.

Similar atmosphere to the señorita at the bistro.

Something exposing in the enthusiasm of the line.

Perhaps you stir at the thought of commanding a fleet,
Ava. Strategy. Salty wood. Sixteen-foot iron bolts

holding fast.

As I said, I was going mad,

but to me it did seem a kind of porn – these exhibits.

The Trust had left me the museum key.

It wasn't open to the public in the winter but, *of course,* I
should *feel free to bone up* on the history of the place.

I liked it.

Slipping out of the studio, through
the drizzle, past the silent cottages, switching everything
on and wandering from tableau to tableau – before
climbing over the barrier and sitting in the corner of the
'pub'.

There in the faux-oil-lamplight, I'd stay very still until the audio went quiet. And look at all the poorly rendered faces frozen in their glee, surprise, sunk glumly over their frothy, solid beers.

One evening the B&B owner rang to check on things, I mentioned the white horse again.

Look, she said and sighed, *I don't normally tell guests this for obvious reasons. I don't even like to think of it. But, I'm telling you – there is no horse. There was a murder in that field two years ago – a local woman – and there hasn't been a horse in there since hers.*

She wouldn't divulge any more.

...the whole thing's been quite traumatic, best not to dwell.

But dwell I did, Ava. Of course.

Sitting against the radiator, I googled it.

Goodgod. So grim.

A local woman killed while tending to her horse.

She'd threatened to report an ex for an assault and he had paid some village guy to murder her.

They'd been caught – the ex and the assassin – both in prison.

There had been a lengthy court case involving half the village – police incompetence, lost evidence, a lucky break that cracked the case involving a hotel's camera being turned outwards for a few crucial minutes while a window was being cleaned.

I fried an egg and ate it in the kitchen.
On the CCTV – the spider's web, now spider-less, was still, the field looked ominous behind.

I couldn't stop my brain, Ava.

Visualising.

The windows all around me were opaque. I thought how easy it would be for someone to watch me eat my egg and not be seen.

I sprinted past the cold, dark rooms as though they might reach out and pull me in.

The next day there was a note pinned to the studio door:

roses are red, violets are blue
I want to be inside you.

The boat lads were all pretending not to watch me find it.

Stifled laughter.

I locked the door and lit the stove.

When the alarm went off, I escaped to the safety of the pub again.

The real pub, Ava, not the tableau – pint of lager, posh Scotch egg.

On my walk home that evening a pine cone struck me in the back of the head. It hurt.

I looked around but there was no one there.

The ground was littered with them.

I had an email from The Trust –

We'd appreciate it if you kept trips to the pub outside of working hours. We're looking forward to seeing the work that you've produced, do send us anything you have so far.

I felt dizzy.

I ordered a mannequin and a wig online.

Some time that night, quite late, a car pulled into the driveway of the B&B.

I held my breath.

A car door opened. Footsteps. Silence. Footsteps. Car door. Engine. And it was gone.

I didn't sleep, went down at dawn.

There was a note pinned to the gate.

The ink had run in the morning's dew,

I could only make out two words:

found you

Ava – what would you have done?
A deep wide nothing opened up inside me.

Not one thought.

Completely numb.

On the path up to the studio a few days later I was
so deep in my emptiness, I didn't see the swan until I
was almost on top of it.

It rose up in the middle of the path,
spread its wings and hissed.

You too? I said,

and walked right back the way I came.

The mannequin had arrived.

I spent the day at the B&B with my paints, a little
handheld mirror – making her up to look like me.

It took a long time to do the freckles, Ava.

I cut the wig a little short.
Then cut my hair.

I carried her into the bathroom, stood beside her in the mirror, both of us naked.

   Well, look at you, I said.

It got dark.

   I kept the curtains closed. Outside I knew the horse was there. I didn't eat. I didn't leave my room. There was a rash on my back from hours against the radiator.

   In the middle of the night there was a sound in a distant part of the house that I'd not been in yet – like someone dropping something small but heavy on the carpet.

   Instinctively I looked to where the mannequin was. She gazed back with my face, placid in the gloom.

   I felt better.

      The morning was wet but brighter.

I dressed the mannequin in my clothes, put her in a bin bag, partly sticking out, and carried her up along the river.

   I thought how mad we must look –

            my double and I,

felt buoyed-up by it,

walking bouncily – big strides – I passed the swan
down in the reeds by the water, it eyed me angrily,
not now, Zeus, darling! I said and winked.

I felt amazing.

I passed an elderly man, out on a bench
facing the water.

Who've you got there? He said as I passed him.

My daughter! I called back over my shoulder.

I took her straight to the museum, placed her in a corner
of the pub tableau – pen in hand, notebook on the table
– she looked frightened.

Good.

I left her there.

The weather was positively glorious now.

Bright blue sky and sunshine glinting off the muddy
banks,

which now seemed edible, I thought.

Martin Cooper glanced up from a
plank of wood he and another man were sawing,

he called out to me,

wait there! One second!

I ignored him.

The masts in the marina jangled in the gentle breeze.

I marched,

imaginary deerhound at my heels.

Talbot! Goodboy! Gooddog!

As I was striding back, the B&B owner called –
she sounded tired. Things with the baby were still tricky,
she needed to stay on.

*Sorry to do this, but there are some guests arriving. You
don't have to do anything, they're regulars, they'll sort
themselves out – but could you let them in?*

She added,

*if you'd like the company, do make a stew, I'm
sure they'd love it.*

I chopped my veg. I braised my beef. I left it on the Aga.

The guests arrived.

A sweet old man; his adult daughter.

Oh, you'll never guess who they were, Ava.

The father and the sister

of the murdered woman.

Really –

as though I'd fallen through the
genres – oh, if only I were a detective, Ava, implausibly
thick moustache, or else a hard-boiled ex-cop *just trying
to enjoy my holiday...*

though there was nothing left to solve.

The case was closed.

Nothing to deduce but awful sadness. The embers
of an anger that couldn't sustain itself.

I can feel her here,

the father told me,

we stay so I can talk to her where she was last alive.

They were good people, Ava.

Nice,

and startlingly open.

They'd only recently been through the trial,

had sat through weeks of gruesome repetition,
which they calmly talked me through.

I guess eventually the words detach – become sayable –
matter of fact.

Were new to me, though –

those words, those things they told me, and the images
they conjured clung to me –

Not mine to feel, Ava,

yet feel I did.

It's like Boatswain's Clench had been emptying me for
weeks, just so it could pour that in –

sudden company
sweetness, sadness, horror and a red wine fuzz,
throat tight with their words, nodding.

That night I saw a clock for the first time since
childhood.

Darling... darling...

Or did I dream I saw it?

It's so strange to be a child and fear time,

don't you think, Ava?

Of all the visions,
it was the clocks that most disturbed me –
not the train which felt inevitable,
not the ceiling coming gently down,
the clocks –

vivid in the dark, they'd rush and lag and stretch
the night as though to say,

no amount of counting, portioning, measuring will
help you here –

all this cannot be quantified
will not be stopped.

The B&B was boiling hot.

The radiator had rebelled against the thermostat.

I touched it, burned my hand.
I threw the big sash window open –

cold air, white horse.

I could hear the father talking
through the window to his daughter.

It was low and tender.

Intensely private.

Dark field, dark road,

the night sky clouded over.

It felt rude to listen, even to the cadence of his words.

I shut the window. Boiled.

Feverish sleep

and in The Big House, there were bodies,
blood, and in my hand there was a knife. My name twin
strolled in through the front door uninvited, shook her head,

What have you done now? She said.

I pushed her to the floor, knelt over her and closed my
hands around her throat, squeezed
hard as I could

but she was unaffected, laughing coldly,
and when I looked again it was my
double – lifeless, freckled, stiff.

Next morning I walked over to the studio
late – exhausted, brain full of the awful things that people
do.

Just as I was emerging from the woods,

I stopped –

paused behind a tree.

Martin Cooper.

Waiting by the studio door, something
behind his back.

His face looked focused and intense.

I watched him waiting,

my heartbeat thick and slow.

I saw the chairman of The Trust
appear across the river, look over at the studio window,
shake his head, walk on.

I waited.

Eventually Martin Cooper huffed, bent down, placed something on the ground next to the door. And walked off quickly.

I snuck over. Full of dread.

I really thought, Ava, that there was going to be a knife, a note in blood, a death threat lying there.

It was a pine cone carved from wood.

The B&B was hot again. *Some problem with the system,* the owner messaged me – there would be a man over tomorrow to sort things out.

I threw the covers off. I tossed and turned. I felt the hours blur –

darling, board that... darling...

The sweet French doctor's voice was on my tongue.

I could hear the distant mutter of the father in the window next to mine.

I really tried to give him space, Ava, but I just couldn't bear it –

too hot, I have to have some air!

I opened up the window

and the cold night rushed inside

and I heard him say, *I love you Deedee*

                and with it came a huge black wave of –
something

      someone

charged
        vibrating

terrible
           it filled the room

it pressed me to my bed –

                  a ghost, Ava.

I know – me neither – it's not like there's no other
explanation – but –

            that wave,

that force,
        that mass –

was charged with human feeling

      really,

    awful – abject – anguished

             and none of it was anything
I recognised as mine.

You must think that I'm mad –

but I had felt the edge of this or something
like it once before, Ava.

When I was small – eleven, twelve perhaps and
my parents went away for a few days,

they dropped me at the house of a family friend,
who had a teenage son I'd never met.
He was at his dad's that week
so I was given his room, his bed,
to sleep in for those nights,

the house was quite chaotic – stacks of
things – magazines, boxes, bits and bobs – all over the
place,

and Ava,

as I climbed into the bed an
overwhelming scent
hit me –

no,

not just a scent,

an atmosphere,

she hadn't washed the sheets.

Now I'm not normally that squeamish, but really, Ava –

it was bad.

An all-consuming sadness
saturated every item in that space –

even the walls,

the carpet, ceiling,

covered in the stuff –

and the horror of the sheets –

the mattress, pillows, duvet,

too much, Ava,

too heavy

it overwhelmed my senses

and immediately
I hated him,

I did!

This unknown boy

who wallowed, brooded, sobbed and raged in that
soft nest –

his body that had left its trace,
its shape there in the bed.

I lay down at the edge of his long indent, utterly
repulsed.

I felt that I was being marked by every fear, every
single dark, disgusting thought this boy had
ever had –

I didn't understand,

nor did I want to, Ava.

If this was boys – if this was
growing up – no thank you!

I balled my jumper up and pressed it to my face
and tried to smell myself instead and cried.

For me. For him. For the room
which was pitlike, cavelike.
Desperate and damp.

You think I'm exaggerating,
Ava, well I'm not –

within a year, that boy was dead.

Yes, dead.

His mother found him in his room.

I think that's what I'd felt – resignation or
resolve. Pure unhappiness.

Anyway,
the big black wave filled the room
and held me down, and shuddered over me for – I don't
know how long – minutes? – hours? –

but that was it –

I'd had enough.

I had to get the fuck out of the countryside.

At dawn I crept up to the museum
through the trees.

My double was waiting there for me – serene,
amid the 'pub' men and their looping chatter, looping
song.

I carried her back
into the studio,
positioned her at the desk with one arm raised
as though waving to somebody across the river.

I lit the stove. Stoked it right up.

The glass got steamy.

OK. I said. And gathered my things
and walked away –

glanced back –

she waved.

I heard the alarm begin to sound.

It's you or me, I said.

I called the owner of the B&B and told her I was leaving,

took the next train home.

So long! Good riddance Boatswain's Clench!

And hello – what – Ava?

But here's the crazy thing –

I waited for the telling-off, the blacklisting
by The Trust for vanishing,

it never came.
He didn't email me again until my time was up.

A brief message just saying that he hoped it had
been good – productive – and how wonderful it was to
see how dedicated I'd become that final fortnight.

I thought, well, just wait until you find her,

but then they posted a photo of my double with the
caption:

We love it when our emerging artists leave us work!
Self Portrait by —

And just like that, Ava, other trusts,
foundations, fancy houses, fancy gardens, small
museums and galleries began to get in touch.

That's how it works, you know –

trustees take the word of other trustees who pass you
onto friends of friends and then before you know it
you're on this circuit – being handed round from place to
place,

and oh – the places that I stayed, Ava!

The storied rooms, the dark four-posters, the
Tudor chairs, the witch marks scratched into the beams!

Manor houses that once belonged to writers,
artists, radical gardeners;

deer parks favoured by long-dead kings;
the site of a Saxon hall;

a graveyard;

a lake house

a former monastery...

soft morning light, wrought iron, my bare
feet on a lawn at night, and owls, Ava,

the owls!

*My sincere thanks to my dear patrons for the owls I heard
and saw.*

And in return for art, I got a room, access to
beauty, history, the freshest air,

no money though.

So between these residencies – which lasted a
week, two weeks, a month sometimes – I was on my
cousin's sofa –

a buyer for a department store, a failed violinist,
an insomniac –

the space in which I slept was the space in which
she was *always* and *very* awake.

Main light.

Infernal, main light, Ava.

I tried to overlap these stays away as best I
could, but week by week, month by month, I was either
in some beautiful house – a guest, an interloper – or
attempting sleep on my cousin's lumpy sofa

while she

paced around the room,

talked anxiously,

chain-smoked,

and played Ysaÿe with a sort of
vengeful vigour.

You play so well! I'd say, my eyes half-
closed. My brain a desiccated mulch.

Everywhere I was slightly in the way.
Everywhere I felt indebted and
embarrassed,

still,

to wander through the topiary at night,
to take a flower, specked with dew and gently turn
its head and gaze into its face,
to don white gloves and leaf the archives...

bliss, Ava.

And a response was all they needed –

something they could put into
their newsletter – proof of artistic nourishment and its
rewards – a modest harvest they could lay before their
funders.

I'm not complaining, Ava.

I mean –

technically I am,

this email is a complaint –

a formal one.

Oh, lodge it, Ava, do.

Goodlord –

and here I almost lost my thread –

carried down that old and winding river – the one you
cannot swim in twice but try a thousand times.

I'm trying now.

Hey, Ava,

here's a question for you –

if you insist I make an account with
Goodlord – this other body, party, platform that you've
partnered with

and I do just that – make an account, enter
my details, wait for the code, input said code into the
little box, and once

I'm registered and ready, this
partner of yours has me click through ads and offers
from *their* partners –

insurance, energy, *etcetera,*

before allowing me to view and sign the document – a
document you could have just emailed to me directly –

what
is being traded here?

Is being sold?

My dear, my darling, Ava,

my little letting love – I'll tell you,

it's my eyes,

MY EYES, Ava.

And I'm lucky,

oh boy, oh wow, oh don't I know how
lucky I am

to have even walked those marble halls! To
have picked an apple from their orchard and eaten it in
their hammock.

To have had a private conversation
with their small van Dyck.

There was a problem though, Ava,

I was greedy.

I was greedy for those spaces – for the panelling, for the
beams, the high ceilings –

the minute I was there I felt
the countdown to my cousin's sofa start

and was restless,

filled with the frantic boredom I had felt at
Boatswain's Clench.

Instead of profound artistic musings, I would
spend the days and nights imagining what it might be
like to own a place like this – to never have to leave.

This tree, I'd think, *this pine tree with its perfect
trunk that glows a sort of golden-pink at dusk as though
it had been set alight*

belongs

to someone.

*This freezing river with its trout and mossy stones
is private – I am here because they've let me in.*

*I can watch the dragonfly now,
but only now.*

Do you understand, Ava?

I couldn't stop glitching over that one same truth –

Goodlord. Goodlot. Goodloan.

Not having.

        Ava, I wasted those visits
wanting,

       Whose woods these are I think I know

         that's Frost, Ava,
you dopey bitch. I'm sorry.

       Today I googled, *is it OK to want somebody dead.*

       The answer: *Absolutely.*

I don't want to pause and watch some other person's
woods, Ava.

       Do you own a house?

One morning while in residence at a calendar house –
you know what that is?

        Your field, not mine – though I highly doubt
you've dealt with properties like those...

        three hundred and sixty-five windows, fifty-
two rooms, twelve chimneys, seven staircases –

       ridiculous really,

        but if you're building a house that
big already – why not add a little number-play, some
architectural symbolism – a paean to the good old-
fashioned Year.

Imagine the listing, Ava!
                    For fans of the Gregorian calendar...

Anyway,

I was roaming this house's kitchen garden –
                    bushiest fennel, neat rows of lettuces,
various onions on the go –

                    my feet were crunching on the gravel
path and

          I was distracted, Ava,

you see, I have these boots, that when it rains,
          make the sound of a very small and frightened
child,
                    only it was raining then
and they were silent,

                    and I was wondering, with growing
concern, whether I had, in fact,
                    marched previously right past a frightened
child or children in the rain,

                    and was remembering the time that I
was walking through a wooded park

one autumn – as quiet and crisp an autumn as I'd ever
seen –
                    and I was feeling blithe as hell, Ava,

          I'd spied this giant pile of leaves in a clearing,

          and I took a running start to kick it –

why?

Why not, Ava – who boxed your inner child and
shoved her in the attic?

And as I reached the pile and drew
my foot behind me and began to kick,
I noticed two things almost simultaneously –

that a way in front there was a man,
holding a small pink backpack, half-hiding behind a tree,

and that a way behind, a woman was
walking absent-mindedly towards said pile of leaves,

and in the instant just before my foot made
contact with the pile,

I realised that there was a child
concealed within.

Far too late,

my foot already on its way.

I kicked it, Ava,

the pile and the child inside.

I never did harm to a living soul!

That's what Tosca sings in "Vissi d'arte",

But how does she know?

How could you know?

I mean,

     I know I have –

                I kicked that child, Ava – it cried.
And then there's that fateful night I – well, no

     something in me –

and I –

       spilled over –

     anger   but clearer, cleaner than that –

        captain's hat,

not yet

     you bitch you can't just – Ava, no.

you bitch you bitch you bitch

Poor Tosca –

     I'd hate to carry the notion that I'd never harmed
a soul – that's too much pressure.

Anyway,

     this is what I was thinking about as I walked that
kitchen garden in the rain – imagine, Ava,

       the space to grow, not one, but several
types of onion!

And I looked down only just in time to see
a bird – medium-sized, brown – sitting in the middle of
the path.

I halted.

I'd nearly stepped on it, it hadn't moved,
it hadn't even flinched.

Its eyes were beady, watchful,
its feathers were speckled at its breast,
it was tucked in on itself – a loaf, a package,

still,
but for the subtle movement of its breath,

and my first thought, Ava, was –

I bet that I can touch this bird.

I reached out for it.

It made no indication it would fly away.

But then I stopped,

why?

why do I want to?

And I realised, Ava, that the way that I was looking
at this frozen, frightened bird,

was the way that men
in cars and on the street had looked at me when I was in
my uniform walking home from school –

like I was a succulent pork roast
and their eyes were dry bread rolls

and they were trying to mop-up
all the juices, all the gravy that they could –

and I'd been eyeing it all that way – the houses,
marble flooring, gardens –
bitter, wolfish, hungry –
mop, mop, mop...

Ever watched the sunrise, Ava, from atop a
famous hill and had to share it with a bunch of other
people?
It's difficult to achieve awe that way.

Bodies jostling for vantage in the not-yet-light,
someone else's dog snuffling at your legs,
a man with poor volume control explaining
dawn –
no wonder people pay for exclusivity, no
wonder people hoard those places for themselves.

I want a sunrise, Ava, I want her rosy fingers to
myself.

Oh perspective, oh sublimity, oh barbed wire
fence post camera broken glass embedded mortar...

What do I have?

I have you, Ava –

this borrowed box of Artex-lined interior,

a minibus-infested window.

chug chug chug...

You know the fascinating thing about this place,
this flat you rent us?

No you don't.

The cul-de-sac outside this window
where the minibuses are is like an amphitheatre –

not in aspect, Ava, you understand,
but sonically –

as in,

sound behaves quite strangely here,

trapped and bounced,
distorted, amplified –

some architectural fluke

the way the houses here are grouped,

walls on walls on walls around
that central car park

and there's a point, a place, just
visible from our window, that is, Ava,
a kind of acoustic sweet spot –

stand right there and whisper –
and I will hear you – crystal clear –
as though your voice were being piped into this flat,

what would you tell me, Ava?
Strange quirk indeed.

Interesting but not exactly
beneficial to our lives.

See, all the drama of the street plays out right
there – exactly there.

A couple arguing at 4 am; the minibus manager's
morning gossip; night-time/daytime drug deals; a local
lawyer talking to a local cat – *see you in court!* She
laughs... and every one of our neighbour's pleading
phone calls to his mother...

that neighbour, Ava,

lives in the flat behind our flat, we share
a wall – he mirrors us, spatially at least –
and in this way
I feel connected to him.

Often I will run a bath and, lying there, will
hear him enter his identical tiled room, kneel down at his
same toilet and throw up.

He's sick a lot.
I don't know why, we've never spoken –

maybe it's the minibuses and he
is my canary, Ava.

At the centre of the car park, he holds his phone
with both hands to his ear –

> *don't say that, Mum,*
> *it's not like that.*
>> *no –*

Mum?

> *Hello?*

Everyone who stands there shifts in tone –
something in their bodies tells them – *you are resonant
– heard, held*, whatever they say or do or think is now a
performance,

and I accept my role as audience.

I even saw a fox run past there once, Ava – it was
sort of yapping, but when it hit the centre of the tarmac,
that same sensation seemed to register, and it backed-
up – the fox – stood on that mark, lifted its head
and shrieked.

These voices, monologues, and screams
have entered my sleep,

street osmosis –

squeezing through the membrane of my dreams
and sauntering through the front door of The Big House.

Goodlord.

Do I even own that house?
Leasehold, I guess.

The Big House never feels like mine,
but if not mine then whose, Ava?

The muted drapery. The polished concrete.
The glass –

am I not both the house, and woman walking through it?

Darling... darling...

and yet I still can't find the basement, Ava,
can't seem to find the stairs
or door –

It's possible there are none.

No way in for me...

and no way out, I guess, for the sweet French doctor
and whatever he has down there.

Buried.

I was buried, too –

sealed into that basement, Ava – for one year.

Listening to the well-lit lives upstairs – their
muffled voices, furniture shifting, the heavy shuffle of that
sour man –

I shudder

at the thought of it –

      and the spiders, Ava,
      the biggest that I've ever seen

and brazen,

      a thin hand shifting on the pillow by

my head.
    It made me ill – that flat,

    I know this

      because while living there I watched
a lot of one specific television programme –

obsessively.

      A programme where a sturdy bloke bought
antiques from France and sold them back in England.

    I'm not sure how many hours of this I watched.
    A lot, Ava. Too much.

    Each episode was the same –

      he'd go to France in a big green truck, trawl
the markets, shops, house clearances – then drive the
things he'd bought back home, where he'd sell them for
a profit.

    Oh I actively disliked it, Ava – hated him a bit in
fact – especially the way he shook hands on a deal, then
looked directly at the camera and said *BOSH!*

I had no interest in antiques
no interior aspirations,

but
for whatever reason, in that concrete coffin
of a room, curtain drawn across the door, across the day,
no company but for the occasional tiny arms of those
portentous twins next door – I'd watch and watch and
watch this man buy and sell and buy and sell

BOSH.

A wardrobe from a château,

BOSH.

a pair of dark green shutters,

BOSH.

a silver butter knife,

BOSH.

a wooden rocking horse,

BOSH.

a chair a chair a chair...

I barely spoke to anyone that year, was working at
a bar across the road, two minutes from the flat.

I'd come home tired at 2 am, sleep until late
morning,

then watch the French antiques programme
until my shift began at eight.

I knew it was a problem, Ava.
I'd started seeing omens in it –
a ladder with no rungs,
a faceless nun,
the word *malle* – trunk –
which I heard as *mal* – wrong.

wrong... wrong... wrong

a man rapping his knuckles on a large
mahogany chest.

Sometimes he'd have the stall owner smell the
money he was offering them, his face made an
exaggerated *oooh*.

If the cameraman was caught glancingly by
some rococo mirror, or bathroom cabinet – I wouldn't eat
that day,

instead I would leave a bag of crisps, an
apple, or some cheese for the tiny gods –

delighted gasp and giggle behind the
curtain.

Poor little twins,

they didn't deserve the weight
of my devotion.

I had to stop, Ava, I knew I did –

I thought that it might happen by default when I
was out of episodes –
there were sixty-five, each one nearly an hour long –

but it looped back at the end
of the final one, began again from the beginning and I
didn't switch it off.

I thought about offering up my laptop to the twins,
but couldn't do it –

instead I forced myself out
and to a party after work, to shake things
up, to check that I was still alive –

and who did I run into at this party,
Ava,

but the curly-headed guy from that awful
gastropub two years before.

Sweet fate, Ava!
Hot and fresh!

We hugged, we danced,
we flirted as we had before,

You disappeared! He said, *what happened?*

Jane, I said mysteriously.

He gave me half a pill, I swallowed it with my beer,

BOSH!

we kissed,

BOSH!

and I thought, *now this is how it should have been before.*

Felt sick with the excitement of it.

Goodsick. Goodgirl. Notdead.

God he smelled so good, Ava.

But the pill was kicking in and I felt weird.

I went outside for air.

Sitting on a wooden bench I let the other people's conversations swirl around me.

A man beside me was gesticulating wildly, cigarette in hand,

I don't know, man, sometimes you gotta eat shit, you know? You gotta eat shit.

A woman sitting cross-legged at his feet, looked up at him,

her eyes were glazed and glittered.

But... she said, *what if I don't want to eat shit?*

And then I felt a pain – sharp – at my thigh,
looked down –

   his hand with the cigarette was resting on my leg,
under it a hole was newly melted in my tights, a circle of
hot pink skin.

   Hey! I said angrily.

They all looked at me blankly, he didn't move his hand
away, continued talking,

      It's not up to you, he said to the girl,
            it's just the way things are – eat up.

         I felt the pain again – another hole.

   Watch where you ash! I said.

He looked down confused, then laughed.

   I felt angry in a foggy way. I marched inside but
like a toddler – slightly wobbly on the steps.

   Watch out, Paddy Ashdown! He called after me.

Inside I found the curly-headed guy.

   Shall we go back to mine? I said.

   Definitely, he said, *just let me say goodbye to Matt.*

   The name hit distantly –

            a lone firework in someone else's garden

thump.

My brain began to ache,
everyone looked unfriendly in the room,
            each person seemed to stare into my face as they
walked past – questioningly. Threateningly.

            The curly-headed guy came back with Matthew –
yes, that Matthew –

                                    whose face I found I couldn't
see as if it had been censored – blurred-out.

Can Matt come for a nightcap too? It could be fun.

            The *eat-shit* man pushed past me roughly,
stumbling for the bathroom.

                        Instinctively, I stuck my leg out and he
tripped, fell into the carpet face first, hard.

            What the fuck? He said his voice all woolly.

It felt good.

            I laughed.

The curly-headed guy laughed too, confused.
Then Matthew was also laughing.

                        Hah hah hah, Ava. I was golden buzzing
and untouchable. Nothing mattered –

            matters...

            Perhaps, Ava,

I might have been more careful with myself,
had I not been living in that basement –
      supreme numbness,

               underling.

What I'm trying to say – what I'm attempting to
explain is why I took them home, Ava – both men.

Agrodolce

It just didn't seem to matter if the *bitter* came along.

      Those diggers, Ava, dug their own graves
         then drove in

were driven
        aren't we all

               and, Ava, in that concrete coffin of a
room we –
      well I don't need to say, do I?

     I woke up very early, sore, head still fuzzy,

crept into the kitchen.

        There was a window in there, the only
window in that flat – it faced a wall so close it seemed
bricked-up,

     but still the light squeezed through, Ava,

I could hear the sour man's hacking cough,
        a pigeon cooing, scrabbling on a ledge,

           I got a bag of frozen peas out of the freezer,
stuffed them down my pants, and stood there
in a daze.

      He wheezed, he coughed again.
           You know what I was thinking about, Ava?

In that greyish light, beneath that house that held three
different flats, three different lives above my own half-life,
a pack of frozen peas betwixt my legs,

      I was thinking of the time an orchestra – a good
one – visited our school on some sort of *outreach
programme.*

        A composing workshop.

We're allocating each of you a musician, they said,

        *we want you to compose something for
their instrument – anything you'd like – and they'll perform it.*

One hour! Then we'll come back and show and tell.

        Ever done anything like that, Ava?

You have to understand that trying or enjoying was a
fault back then. A weakness,

     so it's not like we were buzzing –

chair tipped back, tie short and fat, covert
mascara, lip gloss, gum.

I went to my assigned classroom purposefully dumb.

Waiting for me was a man – large, red-
haired, red-bearded, smiling.

I couldn't see a horn or drum or violin.

What do you play? I asked him and he laughed,

I'm a baritone, he said.

I'd hoped to get the flute, of course.

I could hear the other students in the other rooms,
constructing melodies with clarinets and cellos.

What do I do with you? I asked.

He handed me a sheet of paper with blank staves.

*Just write the notes, and write some words beside
them, and if you want vibrato draw a squiggly line, and if
you want me to be loud or soft, or to crescendo – write it
in, don't worry about the proper symbols.*

He was nice. Which made it worse.

It felt too intimate to put words in this large man's mouth.

I sat, head down,
pretended to sketch out ideas

while he sat at a distance, emanating warmth.

I felt grim and stupid.

The conductor poked his head around the door,

five-minute warning!

I needed words.

I had the exam anthology in my bag, I
opened it at random on a poem – took the first phrase
that stood out –

green tigering the gold.

Neutral enough, I thought –

what could anyone accuse me of liking?
Of yearning for

in that?

With minutes to go I swiftly wrote the line across the
page – just those four words – stretched out
so that they covered all the staves.

A few notes above each word, some scribbles to
suggest dynamics, or effects – I didn't know what I had
made.

Time to go, the baritone said, *have you got
something for me?*

Shame-faced, I passed the sheet to him,

he looked it over, smiled.

We listened to the other students' work –
jolly melodies, brooding trumpet solos, a comedy
bassoon.

When my baritone got up to sing the room went quiet.
Curious.

I sank down in my chair.

His voice hit the *g-r* with force

a sonorous growl

rich and clear,
a shock – like I'd been shaken,
surprise on all the other faces too.

Then he slid
or leant

into the *ees*

beautiful and clean,

the room was quiet in a way I'd never heard before,
the loudest silence –

was it good? I thought.

It seemed much more embarrassing if it was,

and I was now suppressing something –
laughter –

but it didn't feel like laughter – wasn't funny.

          His voice was hovering – both still and not
still – the air was saturated,
                  no, suffused
with it.

          Then over the consonants he went –
skittering like a rock skimming a lake.

          Christ, Ava,

the *O* in *gold* –

                it was like the colour, or the thing but
melted down and pouring, pouring, liquid low, a shine,
aglow...

          I think if you'd heard it too, Ava,
we might not – I might not have to –

          When the boys had left the basement flat,
I put a pan onto the hob and cooked the peas.

          If I'd had a walled garden or a clipped
hedge maze to run through barefoot in a nightdress, I
might have pined and waxed and waned and drowned
myself in the fountain, Ava,

          but there was nowhere for my body to
break into a sprint alone,

              and so I climbed back into bed,

     I ate fish fingers, peas and ketchup,

and I watched a man sell a vintage
bread delivery bike for twice the amount he paid.

You called me today.

That's right.

We spoke – you know this, Ava, you've known this from
the start –

Hi, this is Ava from...

and my blood stopped and I faltered,

...hi ...hello,

you asked if I was having trouble signing up to
Goodlord,

trouble?

you offered to guide me through the process
as though I were some reluctant grandparent, befuddled
and enraged by CAPTCHA, shouting

*WHAT DO YOU MEAN ALL OF THE
CROSSWALKS*
WHY?!

Goodgod there's so much that I want to say
to you, Ava,
but not like that –

voice to voice,

you speaking to me as though we were
strangers

I am – what – to you?
A name, a number on your list of
tenants to *hurry up* that day – a chore, a task – I heard
that in your tone –

I murmured only,

it's not your fault this caught me – I...
You were chewing gum, as if you knew.

What? You said.

I told you that I hadn't signed on purpose.

On purpose? You said hardening your
voice.

I heard a shift like you were putting me on
speakerphone,

I muttered something about *Goodlord,*

linguistic insult... pointlessness,

it's capitalism on capitalism, Ava! I implored.

Not my best, I know, I know – but if you'd only
waited.

You laughed, distractedly,

were making faces for your colleagues – I could feel it.

We're getting deep now, you said sarcastically.

Deep, Ava?

Deep?

I was sick with it. The word.

My voice was very small – you interrupted,
sounding bored,
told me to make the account and sign the
document
and hung up on me.
The anger flooded in immediately.

An ocean turning on a fishing boat – roiling,
rising, preparing
to engulf...
Oh, I've been pacing.
Oh, I've been balling up my hands.
Clenching, Ava.

Oh, I've been breathing quick.

Can barely hold it – this – what? – Excitement's
terrible twin

yesyesyesyes

I nearly called you back,

I googled where your office was,

imagined marching over, imagined –

     No.

           Goodlord

you have no idea, Ava,
who I am –
this rage
this cool
cool rage
I
have
I
had
my
evening
dress,
a captain's hat
a captain's hat
a captain's hat
a captain's
deep

       bass   light dimming   strobe ceiling low
jump   glass warm   alcohol sweetening
      wood sticky   wet towel   laughter
skin tightening brain thinned   knee rising
blood-impact   ring imprint

     tooth   yesyesyesyesyes

Goodgirl Goodgirl fuck you, Ava.

     Three things – lead up to this – to that –

a royal wedding.
                    Some information.
                              A bad encounter.

See, Ava, I was staying with my cousin still,
              when that auspicious royal news came in.

I bet you love them, I bet you fucking do,

                    commemorative mug,
                              tiny procession on your big TV.

                         yesyesyes

              Those residencies in the grand old houses had
dried up – well it couldn't last forever could it?

              Perhaps my covetous heart was showing.
Perhaps the work I made for them just wasn't cutting it,
                         perhaps they saw me touch their bird,

Oh yes Ava, I touched it

                              it was SOFT and real
and scared.

                              And on the day those loved-up
royals wed, I joined my cousin
              and her friends at some
                         vanilla-buttercream street party –

                    bunting – *you call that bunting?* – Victoria
                    sponge, face paint, paper cups of wine.

Oh I was mad bored, Ava,

wearing my most sensible button-up dress with little
daisies on it,

I was restless
reckless,

heard some distant bass

and wandered like a child to the piper,
or a thief towards a window pie –

a rougher street, a makeshift DJ booth,
a crush of bodies, cans and smoke,

that's better, Ava,

it didn't matter that I was alone –
I joined the throng, I bobbed and swayed,
I drank a beer,
the MC's voice was blurry on the
sound system,

a man was dancing close behind me
and then with me
and I danced back

enjoying

that I hadn't even looked at him, had no idea whose
body
I was grinding on,

I'm no Orpheus, Ava, Ava, Ava, whoever
was behind me
so be it!

But then he got a little grabby – course he did –
and the crowd was far too thick to move away,
                    I scanned it for a gap, a friendly face, and
met the eyes
                          of three tall men,
quite handsome, in their forties,
                    tanned and rye and sure,

                                        yes please

they smiled and I mouthed help – ironic damsel in
distress, and they reached over
                                        hauled me, giggling,
through the crowd to them
                                only
                                        the dancing guy
had followed close behind,
                    and the three tall men seemed fine with it – in fact
all four closed in around me quick –
                              as though they'd planned it –
made no sense, Ava,
                    they couldn't possibly have –

                    did they know each other?

was all that I had time to think before the men were on
me – more hands – I felt – than it was possible for them
to have, I thought of Actaeon ripped apart by hounds –
wolf's frenzy – Ava, exactly that – as though trying to pull
off chunks of me – I struggled
                          in the cage made of their bodies – fought
upwards as though drowning, almost broke
free for a second,
                    heard one say –

hold it... hold it still..!

It, Ava?

There were fingers inside me then, I didn't
know which man, or men –

broad daylight, middle of a crowd, a royal
wedding, music –

it can only have been a minute –

the whole thing –
so quick, that I still had on

the smile I'd smiled at them,

I swallowed it – I changed my face,
I fought, I fought, I felt
myself go weak,
go limp, play
dead,

and then a group of women saw me,
shouted at the men, and pulled me out.

I was dazed,

are you OK? They said.
Where are your friends?

I didn't want the fuss,
I shook my head, ignored them until they left.

I wanted to be somewhere else,
I wanted to be home – which home?

I didn't have a key to anywhere – I started pushing
through the crowd,

                              a man – thin face, much
older – appeared in front of me,

        sweetheart, your dress, he said.

I looked down, it was unbuttoned to my waist.

        Thanks, I buttoned it up, still muddled – foggy.

I saw what happened, he said,
        here, take my hand, I'll get you out and safe.

I took his hand,
        he led me through the crowd,
                he was smaller than I was, making a meal
of clearing the way,
        but then we broke out into sudden space and
light,
                thank you, I said,

        he pulled me on still, down the street,

he turned to go into an alley

        wait,

                        I stopped, pulled back,

                come on, he said, *I think I saw your friends*
down here.

                Can you believe it, Ava.

No, I said.

He glared at me, walked off.

I waited for my cousin on her doorstep.

When she arrived, a little drunk, I told her
something bad had happened,

she looked tired,

you're going to tell me you were raped or something?

I shook my head.
I didn't say a thing.
She asked when I thought I might be moving out.

Soon, really soon.

There was another wedding that week, Ava.

The creamy-faced estate agent of my youth

had finally met her match

and I
had been invited to the reception.

I took a train back home – home home, Ava –
the brisk salt air,
the drystone walls,
the scrubby moorland

and its creepy cottages.

I thought I might bump into the slightly older lad
            that I'd been seeing all those years ago –
the paint-flecked one, the one I should have
stayed with maybe –

                        I was excited –

        and he was there, Ava – first person that I saw on
entering the room –

        so strong and warm – the same, it seemed –
unchanged – sturdy as I remembered, boyish still.

        Once, Ava, I asked him if he'd ever had an
existential crisis –

                what's existential? He replied.

        Oh, to be so firm! To live so in the body!

                I'd chosen a dress that said

        I live in the city now.   Hair up.

                        You look nice, he said.

Wine.

Then shots.

        A glass of whisky.

                    Dancing madly with other people's children,
parents, husbands,

a bump

                off the bride's fingernail

a kiss on the mouth
for old times' sake.

           She bit me.

You're a bad girl, she said,

    this is not how we behave at weddings.

         The DJ refused to read the room,
so we shouted until the venue kicked us out.

         A taxi into town – all fun and singing, my
thigh against his thigh – how was he always
    this warm, Ava? Like his body was a battery –
stored the sun.

The only bar still open was Snake Boy's, they told me.

    Remember him? They asked.

    That creep! I said, *how is he?*

    He had quite the little empire now – they said –
properties and clubs –

    still has a kink for secret films of girls, they laughed.

    I asked if they remembered my school friend – if
he had videos of her.

They didn't know – they said – then one turned
from the front seat – no, he definitely did – he'd seen it –
he remembers, mostly because she was so young,

yeah, he said, *felt weird watching that one.*

Someone placed a novelty captain's hat onto my head.

The slightly older guy beside me laughed
the cheekiest laugh,

You look like you could command some seamen,
but then you always did.

I punched him softly in the gut,

I did, Ava, I think I did – I loved him – *goodgod*
goodlord...

The bar was just the same as it had been
before – a little grubbier perhaps – low ceiling and all the
chairs were wooden pallets – unsanded – laziness or
fashion who can say – I can.

My tights laddered the second I sat down

and I remembered
all the morning-after splinters
from before.

Drinks.
Too sweet.

Glasses lined up on the bar.
The clink of smaller glasses domino-ing in.

Wedding drunk is such an ethereal kind of
drunk, Ava.

And I – with no place to live, no jangling
keys inside my pocket to weigh me down – now floating
almost – in my evening dress, in love – maybe – maybe
in love –

Snake Boy hugged me, handed me a drink,

It's on the house.

I wasn't angry. This is important, Ava.
I wasn't angry then.

I took my drink and another and went to find the man –
the love I'd loved and might again – the one who's large,
rough hands I'd seen just now in the taxi rolling a
cigarette and thought – *Oh to be a Rizla in this man's
hands, rolled and wetted with his tongue – that's what I
want* – and he tucked it behind his ear in the red glow of
the traffic lights and *holyfuck*, Ava, my heart – stupid
heart –

where was he?

I ducked down through the low door to the
garden – scrubby plants, big bins –

there,

but locked in close and giggly
conversation with a girl,

I stopped, stood dumbly with the drinks,

and they looked up – him a little slower to draw
his eyes away from hers.

This is my girlfriend, he said,
have you guys met before?

I recognised her then,

the youngest sister of the sisters, Ava,

golden,

blonde,

she looked unsure, then
smiled and nodded,

yeah, she said, *at that old house, maybe,*
out by the docks?

The image of her sitting with that goat, serene,
then nude, entwined, flashed through and stung my
eyes, I thought of him with her, with them – all three – I
wondered if he'd done it even then –

maybe, I said.

His hand was round her waist, flat
on her stomach, slightly gripping in a way that made me
ache,

no no no

sad or sick?

I didn't know,

I felt like I might vomit tears –

I stumbled back into the bar,

Snake Boy was in the corridor by the
toilets talking to a girl the age

we must have been

back then,

so young, Ava.

No no no...

She was laughing,

What do you mean you're going to make me wet?

She said

Like this, he said and poured

his drink across her shirt.

She gasped, looked

genuinely shocked – hurt

even,

he was laughing meanly.

See?

She caught herself,

matched his laugh,

hey, she said, *that's cold,*

and I thought how much better
it would have been

if she had hit him.

The song changed in the bar – fiddles,
and a thumping beat –

> *...if it hadn't been for Cotton-Eyed Joe*
> *I'd been married long time ago*

laughter, stomping, fists against the ceiling

...hey! ...hey! ...hey!

The man I loved and might still love ran past me
pulling his girlfriend by the arm to join the do-si-do-ing,

> *...where did you come from,*
> *where did you go?*

his eyes on her face full of –

...hey! ...hey! ...hey!

Snake Boy was leaning in now, pressing the
        wet, cold girl against the wall
and she looked pleased and ready.

...hey! ...hey!

No one was looking at me.

The stomping was loud, was in my head,

I imagined what it would be like to
hit Snake Boy, to knee him in the crotch, to run and
plunge a knife into the yellow pages, or his torso, or his
neck –

...hey! ...hey! ...hey!

                              and then somehow I was in
front of him – Snake Boy – the captain's hat still on my
head – my hands were on his shoulders, pressing down,
my knee was rising upwards, fast

                              between his legs –

        he crumpled,

                              ...where did you come from,
                                    where did you go?

        he shouted for the bouncer, tried
to grab me but I slipped away and ran towards the bar,

        I was watching myself, Ava,

                like in a film,

                an action film,

        I was – I saw – a glamorous vigilante
                        doling out the just deserts

        ...where did you come from Cotton-Eyed Joe

the audience were with me

                        weren't they?

        Shouting *YES!*

                        Kick him again!
        Claw his eyes out!

The bouncer was there now, making
his way to me through the crowd who were spinning
each other, tapping imaginary cowboy boots, it looked
like he was wading through deep and choppy waters,

...hey! ...hey! ...hey!

Still time, still time,

I looked for Snake Boy, he had
vanished,

two barmen appeared, blocked my way,
they were tall and younger than me – big pumped-up
chests like henchmen,

What did you do that for? One asked.

I smiled sweetly, *I don't know what you mean.*

Still time. Still time.

...where did you come from Cotton-Eyed Joe.

They closed-in, making a barrier with their
arms to trap me up against the bar –

one leaned in really close,

bitch, he said, like he'd been waiting his
whole life to say it –

it was funny, Ava,

like a joke,

I laughed.

The bouncer had nearly made it to me,

the stomping was so loud I couldn't think,

and the sadness in my stomach flipped,
became an icy feeling,

zingy, fresh,

I swung my fist

and hit one barman in the jaw –

nothing.

I felt nothing – no pain, Ava,
no contact, like hitting someone in a dream,

I did it again.

He made a funny sound.

How chic!
I stamped my black stiletto
on his foot – these shoes, the shoes I'd bought to bury
my uncle – apt, I thought –

punched him again.

The other barman was grabbing for my arms and
shouting

you bitch you bitch you can't just –

and I swung for him as well and sort of missed but
with the outer edge of my fist and this big ring that I'd
been wearing hit his teeth – his tooth –

and felt it move,
dislodge I think,

pain at my knuckles,
blood – but his
or mine,
or both?

Really painful, that one –

you fucking bitch, you can't just –

One was shouting, the other retching,
both had bloody lips and chins,

you can't – you can't –

and the bouncer picked me up and
carried me out the fire escape, and boy oh boy oh boy
were there some stars out that night, Ava.

Go home, he said.

Where's that? I asked but he'd already gone inside and
shut the door.

I sauntered off.

I stopped at the kebab shop.

Ate some chips.

And Ava,

no one came for me
or told me off
or called the police
or even asked me *why* – not once,
not ever, Ava,

I picked well.

You understand?

Those men were nothing to me –
sacks of flour

to tire my anger out on –

though I think I broke a finger, Ava,

it was trembling, tender, bruised.

I gently slipped it in me – felt the heat and
softness – pain – imagined I was feeling up the bloody
gap, the space from whence the barman's tooth had
flown,

I came.

I slept.

Guess what.

You've emailed me again, Ava.

You couldn't let it go,

you thought you ought to scare me into

signing – no?

Goodlord Goodlord Goodlord

You want to see me backtrack,

cower, beg –

you said:

*Looking at your file I see we failed to give
an updated rental price this year.*
*Unfortunately, we hold no photos of the
property and I was wondering if you wouldn't mind
sending me a photo of each room so I can assess the
current rent, adjust if necessary.*

What

is the point of you?

What is your job, Ava?

A heady mix of laziness and malice right there,

Goodlord,

You
want photos?

You want photos of this shitty flat so you can tell
me that it's underpriced and I *goodgirl goodgirl goodgirl*

alright

Ava,

please find attached my gaping hole.
A video where I slap myself like steak.

The swollen crack along the worktop, several
photos of the skirting boards, the chopstick that we use
to get the oven going, the carcass of the chicken that I
roasted, basted, ate last week, the toilet bowl, interior
shot, which no amount of bleach seems to un-dirty,
here – the plastic window with its mould, the downstairs
hallway with its mould, yes, painted over, still a mass, a
mark, a shadow, here – the bathroom tiles, some grout
missing, the dripping shower, my arse reflected very tiny
in the chrome, the broken banister, the pale green carpet
with its tea stains, mud stains, jizz stains, some of which
are mine, the rest were pre-existing, no, I couldn't tell
you which were which, the mirror in the bedroom where
I'm posing with a mastic gun that I could press against
your ear or in your mouth and seal you up, the peeling
laminate, the gappy plastic floorboards, waxy grime
within the gaps, the muck and fluff and crumbs and hair
within the grime, the wardrobe with its broken drawer, its
dodgy rail, its wire hangers, bent and tangled, here – a
video of a woman getting stuck and fucked inside a
similar one, though in the caption it says *armoire,* ah ha –
moonlit vintage château fantasy, the open bin, its broken
lid my bitter boyfriend claims that he could fix, the faded
sofa that I guess was plump and clean and red but isn't
now, a thousand arse marks, thousand food stains, few
pulled threads across the worried arm, please find
attached the creaking bed where I have dressed as you,
moved-in that bitter boyfriend, kicked him out, kept his
deposit, har har har, see here – the burn marks on the
ironing board, the cover with its jaunty font that now
reads – *YO   EASE ME UP* – a covert photo of a
minibus driver's flaccid dick, the leaky washing machine

that chants for *georgia, georgia, georg–* and no one else,
the bulky fridge that clunks and shudders as though
coming violently, three bare bulbs, a dusty paper shade,
the final passage from *Our Exploits at West Poley* – no I
can't move past it – shut up – look, those boys succeed,
they fix the river back in place forever, live their lives, feel
fine, but what, you ask – you should ask – of the
neighbouring town, left dry and droughty aren't they
thirstier for having tasted water for an afternoon – fuck
them – eternal bumpkins rasping at the corner of my
thoughts, yes, true, my piss is dark, my lips are dry –
attached, attached – my WANT could drive me to a cave
with some explosives, to your office with a brick, to your
house holding a bottle of white spirit and a match, but
no, but no, but here – have thirty photos of the Artex
ceiling, far too low, too ugly, don't you think, and I read
recently it could contain asbestos, should we test it?
Poison porridge – DON'T be lazy, you, come over, no!
This minute – I will hold you by the hair, face up, and file
and sand and let the dust fall down and seep into your
pores, into your lungs, your eyeballs too, I'll breathe in
with you, Ava, seal our fates together – might just be
benign, who knows! A risk I'd take, I'd taste the brackish
water dripping from the waste pipe if you did it too, oh
Ava, I want to wrestle you beneath the gunnera, and
paint your face magnolia, and lie down on a beach and
tie your wrists with strawberry laces, oh, last night I had
this dream I walked in on the chairman of The Trust, he
had my double on all fours, he called her Talbot, I felt
bad, but then I noticed she was loving it, and with my
face, and when I woke up I was shuddering exactly like
the fridge, *Goodlord Goodlord Goodlord* fuckheads!
What were they thinking pressing send on such a name,
it doesn't matter, unimportant, *NOW,* we're getting deep,
spit that gum out, it's no time for foreplay, Ava,

honestly what were you thinking too, with your *delight,*
your *partnering,* please find attached a drawing of what I
think you'd look like fast asleep and buried like a digger,
Ava, there's a clock – it's at the corner of my vision,
speeding, lagging, you won't see it, but it's there – *still*
time, still time, it says, my captain's hat fits snug, so chic,
there's just no need for any other clothing, so
unseasonably warm these days – *still time, still time,* your
fucking fault – it is – it all is, Ava, *dopey bitch,* if I'd had
water for my mill, if I had grabbed that bird and killed
that bird and eaten it for breakfast – where would I be?
Too late for thoughts like that, Ava, *Goodlord,* no use, no,
shhh, Ava, no need to press reply, I'm here – you see,
you see now don't you, yes, I'm here, we have to board
this train together Ava,

darling... darling...

ACKNOWLEDGEMENTS

This book began life as a short performance piece
written for the Chisenhale Gallery as part of their
programme for Nikita Gale's show, In a Dream You
Climb the Stairs (2022). My thanks to Amina Jama
and Amy Jones who commissioned that original text –
without you this might not exist.

I'm grateful to have radical press Rough Trade Books
behind this – I drunkenly told Nina Hervé and Will
Burns that I was writing 'a very long email' quite early
on and they were immediately on board. Thank you
both for your support, patience, careful editing, and for
applying pressure when I needed it. Thanks also to Kate
McQuaid, my agent Claudia Young, and to designers
Craig Oldham and Eliza Hart for making this a real and
beautiful object.

Thank you always to my friends, my parents, and
to John – who knows not to enter a room if I'm inside
muttering to myself, and who I love.